Coming of AGE

Maria Balatsou

Coming of Age
Published by The Conrad Press Ltd. in the United Kingdom 2025

Tel: +44(0)1227 472 874
www.theconradpress.com
info@theconradpress.com

ISBN 978-1-917673-37-2

Typesetting and Cover Design by: James Sadlier, jamessadlier@me.com
The Conrad Press logo was designed by Maria Priestley.

Printed and bound in Great Britain by Clays Ltd, Elcograf S.p.A

CHAPTER MIRROR

She was very stressed. She had to pretend looking happy and accomplished and composed the whole day. It was Her thirty-ninth birthday. She has been experiencing this as the last year She can be young. The last chance to be really alive! Dramatic, exaggerating, ok, but this is how She felt. A huge burden, a stone heavy stress. A dark door She does not want to cross. Is She turning into that auntie She was always cruel to, anytime the auntie would say she was thirty-five plus fifteen years old?

Middle life crisis at its best! Hardcore, genuine, good quality middle life crisis. Bring it on, as there is nothing else to do, really.

She threw Mark's fortieth birthday party recently and She did not mind. She did not, She does not, think Her Mark is old. She sees a young man when She looks at him. Why is Her mirror telling Her such a different story?

Honestly though, time is kinder to men. Mark's wrinkles are not as defined. They don't seem to destroy his face as much. His gray hair is charming. His body looks so sexy still. Is it really time being so unfair and politically incorrect with women specifically? Why?

Well, looking at the mirror is never easy, let alone the day age is marked. It's marked right there. In the lines next to the eyes. The shaggy chin. The skin that gets dull somehow. She has also put on weight. What is this? It was a matter of only a week of withholding and some exercise and all the signs of sins would disappear. She is visibly heavier now and is impossible to shake it off with just a few runs and the no breakfast rule. The consolation is, same applies to Mark now. They go on a diet together and seems like a months' lasting torture for a kilo or two to disappear. No fun.

[Woman, can you please relax? I am overproducing cortisol here and it's a vicious circle if you want to look fab on your birthday! Btw, it's just a day. You looked exactly the same yesterday when you looked at this glass again, trust me.]

[Brain itself came up with the idea to put Brain's phrases in italics for the reader to easily tell who is who. Brain knows She and Brain are the one and same but wants to emphasise the smart lines and the sober analysis come from the Brain]

She has been seeking advice online - as ever. However, there is so much advice for either the young (who clearly don't need it or would never follow it) or the elder (who might be able to afford it yet are past the time where they care). Late 30s. An in-between. A stage where you do care for what is happening. The unknown next stage is scary, completely unsolicited, unwelcome. She feels completely not ready for anything that is happening. Besides, no one helped Her be ready. Every narrative out there is finish school - get a job - get married - have kids. And then people? There is no full stop after the kids! There is so much more, right?

Anyway, enough with the philosophy. If She dwells

on these thoughts for any longer She will just cry [*and the mirror will not forgive the shaggy eyes, which is the complete opposite outcome to what we have been hoping for since the moment I told the eyes to open*]. Not ideal start of the day. Besides, some little more dwelling on age and time discrimination and any hidden meaning in life and getting older, will get Her nowhere and that, literally, includes the office: She will be late. It's beautiful how life's routine is the comfort blanket that saves Her from life's agony. She pulls that blanket violently, making sure She is completely tacked in. Not the slightest gap: cleansing gel, then serum, then moisturiser, then SPF, then eye cream. Saved. She feels calmer. The bad thoughts hidden under the serum.

She can't help thinking that only so recently She was so contemptuous of Her mum and the size of Her mum's beauty bag. It only feels like yesterday when it was literally a splash your face with some water and if you really feel like it a cleanse and sunscreen. She is already exhausted and make up routine has not even started! She remembers buying make up products younger when there was nothing for them to conceal. They are called concealers for heaven's sake and address teenagers! Really? Conceal what exactly? Nature at its best? Even the cheap ones were effective. Like obviously...

Well, with a rough calculation the first minutes of Her day cost about twenty pounds already. And truth be told these pounds were not spent well. The products are not effective. Now that She needs them to, they conceal nothing. A random stranger on the street will immediately tell Her age! That is not a guess by the way. I random stranger did tell Her age only days ago. The ruthless man who, by fate is still in one piece, said She must be forty! Did he not get the memo that you always deduct 5 years from a safe guess in these circumstances? [Can we delete that thought, in case he actually did?] Regardless... She carries on with the beauty routine. After all, Her soul needs the beautiful lie...

She is done. She now ponders at the mirror. Her eyes are exactly the same overtime. That gaze She remembers. A kind, smart, fun gaze. She has managed to darken them. Meeting the wrong people. Saying the wrong things. More often than not... Her eyes tend to recover. Better than Her skin. Her gaze still signals young and happy. Millimetres away, the wrinkles might tell a different story but when She looks carefully enough, Her gaze is there. Exactly as familiar as it always felt. A continuum. She is there. Looking back from the mirror as if everything can be alright. Can be fixed with a witty joke and a projection of the kindness in Her heart.

Anyway, She is wandering off and She will surely be late. Of course, anyone can be fashionably late in the office on their birthday but would they want to? Trousers (took some time to find those that fit), nice top, jacket, boots. Hair done quickly. Ready.

It's not just the gaze She notices. Her hair has remained persistently difficult to tame since youth. Frizzy, big, curly... She feels comfort. Her stubborn hair is again something timelessly familiar to hold on to.

[*that is half the head almost. We are good*]

Enough! She pushes herself out the door.

She is at Her doorstep. She loves every detail of that building. That apartment. They bought it with Mark. Fairly recently. Extremely excited. It housed [*carefully chosen word, here - ho!*] all their dreams, plans, funs. So promising, so beautiful. She has looked into every detail. Mark was extremely engaged too. They rediscovered each other through picking rugs, making choices or arguing over that vase She hates but still decorates the staircase head.... [*We did not really win that argument, did we? - Yes, not very inventive on that occasion, neither assertive. We let it drop. - The argument that is, cause it would have been effective to just drop the vase, you know...*]

The whole apartment is a blend. Of him and Her, expensive and DIY, pieces from their lives as singletons but which found their place in partnership too. Still, it looks coherent. Looks theirs. No one else could live there. She smiles to the thought. To the comfort of coherence in Her life. The comfort of compatibility. What a value when turning thirty nine...

But seriously, what is wrong with Her today? What are all these thoughts?

Hailing a taxi. Of course She can afford it. Of course She deserves a taxi ride to the office on Her birthday. There is this voice in Her head yelling She should walk though [*we have established who that voice is. The voice of reason and reason only: To begin with, this is the, and if not the, one of the reasons the apartment was chosen in this neighbourhood and costs what it costs. To be close to work, right? So what is this taxi nonsense?? Secondly, a good opportunity to lose some of that weight! Whale!* – oops... Taking a mental note not to allow negative self talk. She does feel incentivized to walk though. [*Reason can be so effective, right? I did not need that second argument. I am not the one calling people names btw. No idea where that came from. Childhood trauma? Have not studied that...*].

She walks.

She notices details on the streets as She does. Colours, shapes of buildings, the little signs of nature still making a mark in modern cities. She starts thinking what this place could look like in previous times. Without human intervention or without as much. She used to do that a lot as a child. Trying to imagine a place in previous times, coming up with stories about past inhabitants of that same place. Their stories, their habits. Their clothes, their means. She has not played that game in years. She has not allowed Her imagination to dwell so freely for quite some time. Wonders where the lightheartedness could be coming from. She feels carefree, playful. [*Like, moments ago we were on the verge of ending our life, having reached its middle... Perimenopausal hormonal imbalance?*] She just smiles, carries on with Her little mental game.

Possibly some of these past humans would worry about life and ageing too. Or not? In past times humans would die so young. You were done by age forty. You can't really have a middle-life crisis in your 20s, right? Decay has not even demonstrated itself. And they were so busy having a dozen of kids from age fifteen. Was that better? Is keeping busy surviving a good way to tackle existence?

She snaps. Her little mind game, fabricating past humans on the spot She is on, did not really go into that kind of territory last time She played it! Brain, enough. Every single thought you come up with today is going to be about age? Enough. I instruct you to think of anything but age today. [*She surely knows this has the opposite effect to the one desired. She used ME to read the white bear experiment*] - That white bear experiment that came out of nowhere made Her think She may have accumulated too much knowledge and rubbish in Her head over the years... Takes a mental note to meditate a little more henceforth. A good way to declutter.

CHAPTER WORK

Walks into the office. She was very excited when they moved into this office. First and foremost there is an excellent artisanal coffee shop at the ground floor of the building, with delicious cupcakes and even more delicious guy at the payment till. It is also a beautiful building. With character. Adds to the neighborhood. Unlike the glass and steel modern building with the weird shape and the many floors, it is kind of art deco inspired but still current. It even has small balconies with flowers. It's cute. On top, the office manager has found a way to convince management to have art on the walls in the actual office! Some of it good some is bad, but the key thing is that the art added the rooms do not feel dry. It is not a place to waste eight hours in a day and leave, neither pretends not to be an office. It simply is a beautiful office. She is very fond of beauty as a value in life. As a means to happiness.

The other weird thing about Her job is that they have no open space. Each employee might not have their own desk but they are in a room, with a door. It's easier to find your way to a call when you are only disturbing just another person or two, and the meeting rooms are not as busy as they get in other places. The most important part, you are not allocated an office so if you don't like your roommates you only tolerate them for a day max. At first, inevitably, little pockets of friends sitting together and mobbing others out were created but HR found its way out: random room allocation the night before. [Let *me step in here as this was in fact our idea. We are HR, or to put it more modestly we are in HR. This was still our idea, no modesty needed. In fact, I have used the eyes to read somewhere that modesty when discussing the obvious is, in fact, stupidity. We did not come up with this notion but we live by it and I like it*].

She has been with this firm for almost ten years now. [*Counting years again???*] She has been happy there. With the ups and downs. Joined as a junior. Seasoned up to a more senior role.

This corporate ladder is quite mapped out, isn't it? There are online tools to help navigate through it. Your parents, older family members or older friends have all done it. They have so much to share. Experiences, pitfalls, the whole suite. It's quite clear a mentor is needed and there is guidance how to find one and engage with them. It is clear what the market looks like, when to reach out for promotions, what the goals are. It is clear there is always the added benefit of growth and learning. And yet, not all climb it the same way and some do not climb it at all. But then there is so much online about failure. How to tackle it, what to learn from it, how to move on. Anyways, She climbed it alright. She is where She expected Herself to be.

Her main concern now is stagnation. She is quite unclear where to go from here. Contrary to how to climb the first steps in the corporate ladder, online guidance once past these first steps disappears. Mentors who have done the whole ladder get harder to find. Old friends or family members might never have gone past those first few steps themselves. She has researched. Extensively. Online guidance stops at age 30. First job, first promotion. Done. On your own from there. Middle life crisis without having become a millionaire? Who cares or dares to guide you through that?

Those who have gone past the first steps, She has no access to them. She follows them on social media and takes a glimpse of the could have but She has no clue about the how. The only path She knows is stay in corporate, with a few moves here and there, retire. That is it. Any voids in creativity and job satisfaction can be filled with a few hobbies or, you know, a kid or two. [See? Our ancestors were covering up with a dozens of kids, our contemporaries? With just one or two. Is surely evolution... - Being sarcastic, Brain? -Yeap! - Very helpful, many thanks - I know you want me to think how to switch off and leave you alone with only senses and feelings. Too bad...]

Her mentor does not seem to know either. It's a shock! It was so clear online She needed a mentor, She tried all that hard to find one and now that She is truly lost and Google is to no avail, the mentor is in the dark! Some optimistic people She has shared these thoughts with have responded along the lines "it's a blessing to have the freedom to chose your next move. To lay your own path and set your terms". But She does not feel free. She feels lost. In the dark. [You made me read somewhere that there is no such thing as being lost. If you know you are in the dark, that is where you are. Somehow that popped up. Thought I should share along with the trivial thought I so much like to share: did we lock the apartment? - Thanks Brain. Insightful contributions. Both...]

She sits on Her desk. Settles in, tidies up. Randomly or not, the algorithm picked one of the nicest ones for Her today. She has a view to the park, plenty of natural light and away from the busy areas, like the kitchenette or the break out area. No clue if She needs to share it today. No visible signs or roommates and it's way past 9am. She will have to share with two more if they show up.

Takes out the laptop and switches it on. She will triage a few emails and go for a coffee. All these thoughts and philosophy made Her walk straight into the office in the end. She can't believe She forgot to grab Her flat white! All thoughts parked now. It's Her birthday. She does not need to figure it all today. Easy.

Quiet morning email wise. Some huge retails know it's her birthday and offer 10%. Sweet. She might grab the opportunity from some of those emails but most seem to end up in the bin folder. Real humans-wise, most colleagues don't know it's Her birthday. In Her first ever job as an intern, there was the intranet with everyone's birthday meticulously logged in so there was this OCD ritual with the fake excitement, the card and the cake every now and then. There was the lonely spinster focusing on this too much and that terrible person who insisted we buy expensive gifts to the boss. She remembers the cynical colleague, close to retirement, commenting, if you get the boss expensive gifts it implies you don't need a raise. That was the end of it. Thank God.

This company is rather normal. With normal-ish people who have lives and come here for the paycheck. This is what kept Her on for so many years. Not that She likes it so much but the fear of not finding normal again out there has definitely kept Her put. She packs to make it for that flat white. The crowd of these normal people will start flooding in. The quiet will disappear and the time will start ticking differently until 5pm.

Off to the kitchenette.

Pours the coffee. It's thankfully descent. She could not have stayed 10 years otherwise. A feeling of panic settled there for a moment. [*We need to go to the coffee shop with the delicious guy at the payment till. Hello?? Hello? What is this kitchenette turn of events?*] 10 years. What did She do? Just consumed those in emails and office routine? The panic escalates. She might even get tearful. Remembers She thought only moments ago she does not need to figure it out today. Relaxes. So comforting. She thinks this will surely lead Her to make the same thoughts when She will be in this job for 20 years. "Damn you brain. Let me be happy. It's my birthday!" Confused if these thoughts are meant to be healthy alarms or onset of depression pours the coffee. This is a waste, of course. She will surely make Her way to the coffee shop at the ground floor of the building any time soon regardless.

Gossipy Miranda approaches. She has an involuntary feeling of trouble coming. [*Associations these are called? I remember reading it somewhere. So sexy this gossipy Miranda. Stating the facts. Don't come at me. We look good too. Different but good. We got this!*]

- I hear it's your birthday. Happy birthday sweetie [*you know the tone. How this "sweetie" comes out of people with such bitterness....*]. What is the plan tonight? [*no genuine curiosity detected here...*]

For the milliseconds before She fathoms an answer She thinks:

Is Miranda fishing for an invitation somewhere?

Is she only interested in calculating my age? We tend to throw bigger events on round figures. It can be inferred from a casual dinner reply it's not the 40 yet.

Is she opening up the floor for trickier questions to follow and more information and gossip to gather?

Is an honest reply about plans the best?

- Just casual dinner at home. Mark is cooking. He is making the cake too.

For the milliseconds after she has given this reply she thinks:

[Do I sound old?

Do I sound miserable?

Should Mark have put together something more interesting?

Could it be the case he has?

Why am I in the kitchenette?

Where did Miranda find this awesome skirt?

- Oh that is lovely. We know what excellent cook Mark is.

In the next milliseconds She brings to memory some of Mark's top recipes. Lucky Her. She also thinks: (impressive that her mind can drop the food memories and think the list below)

Does Miranda really know Mark is an excellent cook? How?

She is lucky, right?

Is Mark cooking Her favorite or will try to impress Her?

She vividly remembers Mark offering to cook and do the cake. Right? Or she ends up with pizza and a candle on a muffin tonight? Can She still claim to be lucky if so?

- Yeah, he is good.

- He has an insta page with pictures from everything he makes, right?

Now She is quite positive She did not tell people in the office about that page.

Is Gossipy Miranda just trying to get on Her nerves?

Could it be Mark told people in one of those plus one office parties?

When will people realise plus one corporate events need to be banned?

She is in HR, She can suggest the ban.

Is Miranda (ten years her junior by the way) trying to say something or just trying to make Her jealous?

If Miranda was not ten years Her junior and sexy would She still have these thoughts?

- Yeah yeah. He has put some effort into that. He would be happy if everyone I knew follows that page. The more followers the merrier. You know how insta works.

Well, does she? She is probably using TikTok and checking Insta if she is really into older men. [*Or our man* - Thank you Brain ruining my birthday with agony now. Really needed this]

These days society is ranking us with age on top of the money and the race and the family background and the schools. You are on facebook, you are really an oldie. Instagram, you surely have some grey but you still catch up. TikTok - young. Full stop. Clear. She has tried to use TikTok. Refusing to claim She no longer belongs in the young generation. Fail. She thinks it's silly. That is the key. Young people find it cool. Were She young She would do. She finds it silly. She is old. [*We are now serious and conservative. Just stating the facts. Miranda is young, sexy and on TikTok.*

- For the love of Jesus Brain!]

- Well, happy birthday and have fun tonight. Take care of that Mark. Rare kind these days.

(Quiet thought: What a bitch!)

(The office appropriate reply: - Thank you. Will do.

(The tempting to offer reply: Hope someone like Mark lays eyes on you too someday)

[*I pick the office appropriate and make mouth say it and taking notes of the rest for when we meet the besties*]

These tempting-to-offer replies tend to settle the feelings on the spot, feel like an much needed defuse to bubbling anger and have given Her some of those wrinkles She saw in the mirror this morning. The so-tempting replies tend to lead to regrets. Once She realised, She has been fighting hard the impulse, thinking the glow of Her skin to keep Her incentivised to shut up every time. Like now. [*Inner calm and diplomacy, the secret to better skin? A business idea that will get us out of this company?*]

EMAILS

She triages emails. Same task every day in the last 10 years. In between She also triages her personal email account. It's a funny feeling this. She always has a secret hope one of those emails will prove life changing or something. Her hope is almost comical. But is there...

She checks if there is anything really urgent. Happily it's just the usual. In most She is cc'ed. Meaning She can ignore until it becomes urgent. That is a real sign of seniority in corporate, being cc'ed. She is supervising, not taking onboard the task Herself. CC = Someone else needs to prove to Her they can actually perform the task. Or someone simply wants to share responsibility. Both, signs of seniority. Clear signs. She smiles at the thought. Not sure if She is proud or amused.

She realises that other than the kind and gentle retailers and their discounts, She receives no happy birthday messages. No one knows about Her birthday? She has a calendar buster at 3pm... Maybe people are looking for an excuse to a cake and to finish early after all. Maybe She gets a card with "Happy Birthday" written on it a few times. No real creativity in wishes when there is no love... [*Alarm! We are slipping into the philosophical again! -* Thanks Brain...]

Her kindest colleague, who usually demonstrates a strong desire to escape corporate life, would go and pick the card up. Their perfect excuse to escape the office. There is usually, also, the foodie - baker - show off - bored-at-home who will have a go at the cake. At Her first job that would be a girl who really knew how to bake. Not the case in the last years... [*Oh boy, one more reason to skip the sugar.*]

People's reaction to birthdays really varies, She must admit. She can't be bothered truly if Her colleagues will, in the end, engage in the the cake and card routine, but She somehow feels, it will better mark the day if they do. On the other hand, Alice from procurement specifically asks for her birthday to go unnoticed. She will not tell anyone before hand and either pretend sick on the day or say she needs to leave early for a very sad reason or simply work from home. Weird. No cake benefit to the team from Alice's aging. Is Alice in denial about aging? She does look youthful somehow. [*Could that be her trick? -* Funny thought Brain, thank you]

The men also don't care that much She notices. It's the women that make a fuss out of their birthday [*in which case what is wrong with Alice?*] and the birthdays of others. Men tend not to be the ones caring for that card and the cake and the secret emails. They are more relaxed about it. They are more relaxed creatures, in fact. After office drinks, a good laugh. That's it. Consistently that is it. Irrespective of age. She should take notes of these thoughts. She should try the relaxed beer after office and the good laugh for a change maybe.

It's almost midday. She notices another sign of seniority: as She was going through life's challenges and pressing questions, Her corporate auto pilot Brain sorted emails in the background. Urgent matters identified [*none for today*] and sorted out in the to-do list by way of importance. The easy ones first (a classic trick to feel the list is getting shorter quickly) and then the bulky ones that will need time. The bulky ones will have to patiently wait for after the cake. The sugar kick will help problem solving. Always has. She thinks of the gigantic bucket of ice cream that has solved so many of her love problems. [*Not. Definitely not. If felt soothing and instead of solving any, in fact only added a problem: lose weight -* Brain! You are taking this too seriously]

She can vividly bring to memory Herself crying, an empty bottle of red wine somewhere in front of Her, Her friend who would have come to the rescue, impatiently and judgmentally listening to that same line of events about Mr Loser number whatever, Bridget Jones first movie in the background and a gigantic bucket of cheap quality but delicious ice cream. A consolation, an anchor, a reminder there are sweet moments to life, literally. Sugar. Problem solver. Consolation. She starts thinking about cakes and muffins. She also starts remembering things and events about Her and Mr Loser number 3, and then number 4... She struggles to understand why on earth She would be swallowing all that ice cream over them [*another sign of seniority ...*]

CHAPTER MANAGER

She managed to hold Herself. She does not need more than a couple of slices of cake today and at least two occasions where She will have cake are planned for later. She can't take all the credit for Her self-control, though. Alice from Procurement and Norunda from marketing really helped Her not to make Her way to the coffee shop with some office related questions and HR matters. [*I struggle to say we are grateful or happy here, but I admit it was for the best*]

She is back at Her desk. People come and go. Some share a happy birthday. Some don't. They don't know, they don't care or they just did not bring their whole self to work. Just the robotic task performing version, the one with no feelings and acknowledgment of others as humans. [*Since we do work in HR, shall I come up with a bring your whole self to work policy?* - Not in the mood for corporate sarcasm right now Brain, thank you]

For some, though, it is a clear blessing they did not bring their whole self to work. Today or any other day. Their unprocessed anger will surely result in casualties so maybe their cynicism or withdrawal are actually welcome alternatives [*this is a very interesting topic for a thesis and, no, dysfunctional emotional management is not the best alternative. If we are really interested in this topic, by the way, why don't we go back to school and shine?* - That could be a very interesting thought Brain. Keep in the forehead or the cortex it should sit in. I don't know the terminology, you do - *Sure]*

As She goes through these thoughts, notices Bob the Manager making his way towards Her. Bob is one of those office personas that come from a different era. Not sure why he works to begin with. Classifies as a boomer. Not a bad person. Not at all. But somehow aloof to human nature and feelings. As long as he looks good (and he will walk the extra mile to look good) and collects the paycheck nothing else matters. He will create the silos that serve him, the drama that suits him, promote the version of the truth that propels him and as long as someone is no obstacle to that, he will be friendly and pleasant.

If you have not guessed by now, he is somewhat average in built, figure and handsomeness, however for some reason he counts average as extraordinary. Deep down, She thinks, he knows, hence compensates his averageness with flamboyant and expensive additions to his look. Thank God there are limits to what a man can wear in the office, otherwise everybody would have to tolerate his authentic looks. The Christmas and the summer parties have given him the opportunity to show his genuine sense of style and to everyone else in the office the opportunity to be dazzled. Gossipy Miranda has always been playing the office joke, what he would wear on a date... [*She is into old men, come on, what more signs do we need?* Gossipy Brain, behave!]

He has been with the company for more than 20years now. Too expensive for the company to push him on a new path, too comfortable to adjust to anything that has happened in the last 20years, too demotivated to remember the names or other details about the people in his team, who arguably have been changing. He goes to the gym a bit too often and is convinced his choice of cologne is perfect [*not!!*] He has a bizzarly shaped ring on his ring finger possibly to hide the wedding ring underneath for any easy victim. Always well groomed. Always cheerful and smiley, sees everything as "simple". Truth be told, when he says "but this is simple", the most obnoxious if not plain stupid things come out of his mouth.

He also likes meetings. She thinks he likes the tone of his own voice. Anyone below him in rank is to be ignored or, as a minimum be treated with contempt. With the C-Suite, of course, he will push himself to remember a favorite color, restaurant, kid. This is tremendous effort for him. He seems well rewarded for his efforts [*I know. We work in HR*] just not sure what efforts exactly. [*If remembering colors and kids' names cuts into promotion then, problem solved I guess. Or problem identified, if I may*]

Bob walks towards Her. Clearly locking eyes with Her. Shapes a fake smile on his face. Says nothing regardless.

- Hi Bob (you tend to speak first with Bob and acknowledge him - *Isn't that what we do with Kings?*)

- Hi... I understand you are the birthday girl (bizarre smile and gaze continue) [*Impressive, he knows, even more impressive he bothers to mention!*]

- Well yes that's me (not sure why She softened Her voice and acts a little childlike on this occasion)

- Well, happy birthday (as expected no mention of Her name)

- Thank you.

- Look, saw your calendar is free in an hour. I am away next week. Can we catch up?

- Yeah, yeah sure [*Manager's request for a catch up is usually trouble? Let me give a signal to amygdala to release some panic hormones. Party time!*]

- Great, please send me a calendar invite in an hour and we chat then

- Yes, sure. Thanks [*why are we sending the invite? He can't be bothered or the boomer is struggling with the tech?*] Part of that thought seemed quite amusing to Her. She smiled. He did not notice. Moved on already.

{an hour and a calendar invite later}

In all old movies and sitcoms the manager have their own room and you knock on their door to meet them. Bob the manager, has tried playing the I have too many confidential calls card to the C-suite for a private room, but since we are not in old movies anymore, he is still booked in a shared room, same as anyone else. Everybody still knows that you need to find a meeting room to meet Bob the Manager and so She did. Eventually, he is in the meeting room first so She did have to knock on a door to meet the Manager!

[*We are so proud of those office arrangements. Open space and flat hierarchy is the new norm. We all know that addressing people by their first name does not really establish any lack of ranking between them, and politics still flourish in open space as they did behind the closed manager doors. Open space is only noisy and cheaper and does not foster collaboration, only causes headaches because people feel the need to be on guard all the time. Or, those that should have been locked away are in plain sight offering their voice, body odour and bad jokes to everyone* - Brain, we still work in HR. What sort of political incorrectness spree is this? - *Just stating how our idea on office arrangement should concur the world.* - Noted]

In any case, Bob the Manager cannot settle (or adjust) to any new norm. And no matter how the C-suite told him off, he keeps fighting the battle for his own corner desk. She feels like a movie star. Knocks on the door and will meet the Manager. Possibly Bob's flamboyant blue suit perfectly paired with animal print shoes, yellow glasses and orange socks adds to how theatrical it all feels.

Was he allowed, he would have framed a picture of the wife and kids along a Benjamin plant in the corner. [*Actually, in other companies people like Bob the Manager who work in real open space tend to book a meeting room all day and use it as their room! Everybody would know about it and the room still persistently shows up on the drop down on outlook calendar as an option to book it. Rookies tend to get it wrong, which to some seems like an extremely funny incident. Just saying*]

She remembers the time when a rookie booked a meeting with Bob the Manager and made it in 2' early – eager as only rookies get. The rookie started the call with someone not as senior as Bob the Manager, as opposed to waiting for Bob to start the call. Bob came out of that meeting with a hilarious look on his face, but She must admit he was rather composed. He kept it professional, even though the color of his face did match the crimson pair of shoes he wore on the day. Those shoes were usually perfectly matched with a pair of crimson glasses. By the way, Bob the Manager has no eyesight problems.... For some reason She cannot remember any other details about the rookie, neither can bring to mind any memories of him after this incident...

- Hi, ready for our catch up? [*we address Bob the Manager first, remember?*]

- Yes, yes of course. Please take a seat (no mention of Her name still)

- Birthday small talk for about five minutes. She is getting stressed and perplexed.

- Well, good good. Hope you enjoy your cake. So wanted us to catch up because, I think I mentioned I am off next week so won't make it for our 1:1.

1:1s are meetings between a manager and a direct report to discuss needs and progress of the latter. Bob the Manager enjoys all meetings and the sound of his own voice so 1:1 are all about him, his accomplishments, his family, weekend plans and a complaint how busy he is. He will purposely dedicate the last five minutes giving the floor to questions and concerns.... He seems to come straight to the point a bit early this time. She panics. She scans for any valid reason to. She is sure She is safe. She is, however, feeling Her palms sweating a bit. For God's sake, She is a seasoned professional! [*ha! Now we are proud of our age all of a sudden?? -* Shut up Brain! Let him speak]

- yes, you mentioned.

- Well, I don't have much to report and if anything comes up we can discuss during the next 1:1 after I am back, right?

- Of course. (Feeling stupid for the sweating palms. A classic low self esteem reaction. Ridiculous of Her. Re-reminds herself not to negative self talk yet finds it impossible not to carry on in the present moment).

- So will keep this one short and sweet (Got it. He needs to leave the office early. He is only focusing on his holiday plans for a while. Clear. She should have expected this, instead of panicking because for the first time in history, Bob the Manager is jumping straight into the meeting agenda as if he cares what the meeting is really about).

- No problem

- I was at the latest board meeting (extra pride

in voice and gives Her that -you do know I am important kind of stare) and this company is proud to be on the cutting edge on certain HR matters. You know that right?

- Yes, that is true (to a certain extent lying here by the way. Cutting edge is an exaggeration. A lot of ideas that truly matter to improve people's lives out there and which She has been fighting for, have not been taken well by the Board. In all fairness She doubts the Board ever got to listen to them. Board members are usually clever people with experience, they should have taken onboard at least some of them. They like good ideas. [*Are we a little naive here?*] These are the genuinely invested board members of course, as there is this other version too: money collectors who come to board meetings for the sandwiches).

- Well, yes yes. We are a great company.

- (Nods) [*Excellent alternative. There is so much words can mask after all*].

- It was discussed, and I must admit I was pivotal in bringing this forward. [*is this a cue to clap? - Brain don't dare to give that order to the hands!*] I am convinced that we need to introduce certain policies for our employees to adjust to modern world and foster diversity and inclusion.

- That is brilliant! (For a moment there She naively believed this company would introduce work from anywhere or same parenthood leave for both mothers and fathers...)

- I know. This is so exciting. Well, we want to consider including a line or two in our policy for menopause. Can you pick that up please?

In the milliseconds (to be honest Her shock may have lasted a real whole second if not two) before She answers She thinks:

Menopause? Why Her? Is She vividly looking that old now?

What does Bob the Manager have to do with Menopause and how could he have been pivotal to anything that has to do with it?

Menopause is to be squeezed in a few lines in an existing policy?

Does She fight the battle to bring to this issue the attention it deserves now? At all?

Luckily, with age (sometimes) comes diplomacy. Her brain is now trained to pick one of the safe phrases that buy time in a conversation She would rather not have but must. [*See, we get better as we age. Like wine* - Shut up Brain - *this part starts getting tricky. I am still the one running this conversation with Bob the Manager you know* - Hilarious. Like nightmares. You create them and still you get scared by them! She read that on facebook one day and was taken aback and burst into a laugh. She risks laughing at the thought of it all now. She mustn't. Yet She should. *Facebook is Meta by the way, let's get used to it at some point or we sound too boomerish*]

- Well, that is really a step to the right direction. I am not ready to offer brainstorming right now though. I need to do some research and all and come back with something concrete.

- No worries, my dear. Take your time. I don't expect you to know it all right now. Put something together, send me an email and thoughts and suggestions and we take it from there.

He is already standing up, can't wait for the meeting to end. He can't know anything about the subject by experience, even though he is past it, age-wise, and clearly cannot be bothered either. Bob the Manager called a meeting for two lines in a policy. Does Bob the Manager still consider Her junior? Is he a sexist? Is She overthinking this? Did he just want to have a meeting booked in the calendar on the day he travels?

- Ok great thanks. Will do. I don't really know that much about it from experience you know.

God Knows why She felt compelled to make that comment. 10 years earlier She would not have had, right? She would think it's irrelevant to Her. Same as death. Young people don't think about death. Young women don't think about menopause. Bob the Manager just nods. Says bye. She wishes him to enjoy his holiday. She is already looking at his back. Meeting adjourned.

Back to Her desk. Perplexed, insecure, sad, scared. She surely feels stupid [*Hello! No negative self talk, remember?]* It took a 10' interaction and the word menopause to invoke so much. She is not ready for it. She does not want it to happen. Not now. She is so young. She is only just starting to enjoy life. She feels as though She will be terminated. As a woman. As a potential mother. As a creature. She is almost nauseous. She can only think of menopause as a mini death. She cannot control it, She cannot escape it. It will be awful, for Her body, Her life, Her man. Can't science deal with this in the next year or so?? *[Panic seems established. These feelings taking over us, do get on my nerves. .. and I happen to be full of nerves...]*

CHAPTER THE HAVE KNOWN YOU ALL MY LIFE FRIEND

She needs consolation immediately. Her breathing changed. She surely cannot stay in the office any longer. She might snap at the next person who will say happy birthday to Her. Especially if it is a woman under 30. There are quite a few around. She can't risk it. Statistics are against Her. Grabs Her phone and Her jacket and She is out the door.

She has quite a few friends. Some change over the years and give their places to new ones of course. As She grows, as She changes, friends no longer stick as easily. She thinks people start changing quite dramatically after the age of thirty. Life's realisations and lessons come at tectonic rate, at least to Her they did. So a friend that was alright or fun at college, is just someone She has nothing to say to now. She has become more selective, more impatient with incompatibility and less tolerant. She needs things from friends and She will no longer stick around if She does not get them. She realises what She has to give in a friendship and She is not willing to waste it. Conflict proved an ingredient in Her life with a fun trajectory: in Her teenage years there was so much inner conflict. Unprocessed anger, incomprehensible even. Progressively, the calmer She would grow internally the more conflict She would experience externally, with others. The incompatibility would manifest quickly and the need for barriers would be non negotiable.

Her most classic scenario for a friendship to terminate is when the friend would marry someone not compatible with Her. Most usually a sign the friend was never really compatible with Her in the first place. Possibly, just a circumstantial friend as She calls them. People bond for all sorts of reasons like they work together, share a hoppy or just share a status. The girl from the office it's easy to vent with. The other single girl that likes to hang out to cool places. That girl from the dance class that lives nearby and they come home together. The girl that is going through a similar kind of misery in life and you know, misery likes company they say. [*They are right*]. These friends disappear quickly. On one occasion or two She would get a friend back when the friend would realise they are not in fact that compatible with the man they married and the friendship would rekindle. [*Sad but true...and possibly a sign of compatibility with the friend in the first place after all*]

She has been blessed with two very real friends though. She can't even imagine how lucky She is and not sure whom to thank for such a blessing. She has the I-have-known-you-all-my-life one and the-closest-to-her-heart one. The have known-all-life is a sister kind of friend. That person knows the ins and outs of Her life, family and journey. They saw Her grow and did not get bored nor scared. They forgave the person She were, love the person She is and likely they look forward to meeting the future kind of person She will become. Like sisters, She does not really like back everything about them. They are however so bonded, so invested in. There is that love between them, deep, routed.

Anna is that friend for Her. Their parents were neighbors before they were born. They went to the same school. They stuck during college even though miles apart and the rest is history. She remembers how stressed She were the summer before college. So scared of the unknown, and even more scared knowing that whatever lies ahead will be a different experience for Her and Her friend. It was so sad. They would not experience any of this huge events together. That was in fact the scariest bit. They would live in different cities, meeting different people. They could exchange information about all that but the one would not meet the annoying or fascinating person they would talk about. That summer was the most emotionally charged and perplexed and sad three months ever. Then that very unknown was not as scary after all, it was a mix bag of good and bad, sad and funny, interesting and boring as any of the stages they both would fear so much in life. They made it through. She feels happy they did. She is not sure how they made it though. She has come to think they simply both wanted to. Sometimes that is all it takes for two people to do great things together.

Anna knows how ridiculous She was as a kid, the pranks classmates played on Her, how justified it is She is eternally angry at Her mother. She does not need to explain much, Anna either was there experiencing Her past with Her or is just filled in with all chapters, all details, all dreams, hopes and tears. Even if She tried, She can't keep things from Anna. Anna has so much data by now, she reads through. Besides, Anna wants to know. Cares.

Anna recently accepted a job in the same office complex as Hers. This is not the miracle it sounds. Half the population in the city work in that area. That is how big cities are designed. Yet, is counts as a blessing as out of that half city population She craves for Anna's company and now She can quickly and easily access it.

Anna also has a very flexible job. As long as she is not in a meeting she can do what she likes. She has worked hard, she is very successful and very sought after. She has a thing with people, dazzles them immediately. She is that tall, slim, sweet face, sweet manners, patient, clever person you somehow want in your life. Her sparking green eyes, her effortless smile, the beautiful long hair (she never changed haircut since childhood). She carries a warmth, she is non judgmental, she keeps people around her at ease. And people around her open up, want to spend time with her, want to spend money on her. It is magical. It works every time.

She has always hoped she could dazzle people. Play with them. Instead, She is the insecure kind of persona, always busy measuring herself up and against. When She actually meets new people She is so busy comparing, She then forgets to actually meet them. Like instead of saying an honest hi to coworker Sam, She just checks if Sam is better dressed on the day. She might forget to even spark a conversation or She might miss the cues Sam might have sent Her to start one. She only sends out the cues for Sam to better avoid Her. Some people have managed to ignore Her insecurity, see through it (what She, herself cannot) and loved Her regardless.

Anna has seen Her. Anna loves Her. That is Anna's magic with people: Anna accepts them and makes room for them in their most genuine shape and form. Anna will then have the opportunity to disassociate herself form jerks without reminding them they are jerks or to keep herself close to the good ones. She, on other hand, the complete opposite to Anna, is so busy with Herself that allows room for the jerks or does not leave enough room for the good ones. Her insecurity might even lead Her to associate with the jerks just to prove a point, like how big of jerks they are and She is not. [*Glad we are doing these realisations now cause I always wondered what we do wrong with jerks!*]

She rings Anna straight after the meeting with Bob the Manager. She feels old, helpless, closer to death itself. Anna is Her age, does she feel like that? They have not really discussed anything around menopause yet. Anything around aging. Sex, restaurant, dresses and drinks are still on the agenda on every call for God's sake. Why would they? Anna is married. Mother of 3. She can't possibly be bothered about menopause. It's only when you want to have kids still that you worry about these things, right?

She cannot tolerate Herself whilst listening to that classic ringing sound of a phone call. Fiddles with hair. Bites a nail or two. Finally Anna's voice. A consolation, a ray of light!

• Hey

I am so glad you picked up. I am doing my water

cooler phone call cause something really uncool has just happened.

Ok, hi to you too.

Oh come on. We don't have much time and I need to spill it all out. Are you having a good day though or we need to pick up on something more important happening in your life?

No same old for me. Tell me. But glad you asked about my day. Seems like you are less of a selfish bitch now.

They both laugh. Anna's directness has been bitter at times. But some times it has been useful, healing or awakening, if not all three.

- Well. Bob the Manager.

- Noooo.

- Yes.

Again?

Yes!

Okie. What did he do this time?

He mentioned that as part of our brilliant diversity and inclusion roadmap, I should add a line or two in our policy about menopause!

That is in fact brilliant, I must admit.

Anna!

Anna what? Is this worth a panic phone call?

What do you mean?

He has done so much worse. This is like BAU for your job? No?

He wants me to do menopause, on my thirty-ninth birthday!

Ah, now I get it. He pulled the wrong string, on the wrong day for the wrong girl... Did I say happy birthday by the way? Shall we hang up and I give you a birthday call? It should fix your mood

That would be lovely. Can you make it that menopause will not reach me before age fifty-five, or even sixty please?

Haha - I might have some trouble delivering that, but will definitely incorporate in my birthday wishes to you

You are still making fun of me, right? You don't get what made me snap

No honey, I do. However, the bright side, menopause deserves a policy in its own right. A couple of lines as he puts it sucks, but at least there is the acknowledgement. He also realizes this is a diversity and inclusion issue. It's not ideal, but this is Bob the Manager. At his level of emotional intelligence, what you are sharing is just so optimistic!

But why me?

You can't be taking this personally, are you?

Of course I am. All I can do is the associations in his head! Woman close to 40 - menopause expert - let's assign this to her

I really find it difficult to believe his mind went through the association to your age. He is probably completely oblivious of how old you are, when menopause really kicks in or what it actually is in full grasp and just wants you to do your job

[*Our wise friend Anna has a point here, don't you think?*]

You are probably right

Babe, it's your birthday. And your thinning hormones are not helping you think straight. It's just the company doing the right thing (it could be for the wrong reason) and he picked you without even realizing any of what is going on in your head.

You think so?

Positive

I am so freaking out with growing up

It's not easy for any of us sweetie. Not even Bob the Manager

Somehow I think if I had children already I would be in a better place. I guess motherhood keeps you immune from this panic. I am alone on this.

Wait a minute. Are you inferring, I don't care about menopause because I already have children?

[Oops! We are mean, immature and naive]

- Oh I am so sorry. I guess I said something stupid.

- Anna has stopped listening. She carries on furiously. She can't believe her friend is that naive or self-centred.

- Excuse me?? Do you really think that having kids takes away the anxiety? In a way, they, actually, make it worse. You see how young they are and compare. Or you see how they grow day by day and you are reminded that time flies. You have them in your life and they take front stage and you realise you are getting closer to an end! And what if I wanted a 4th child? And what if something happens to my man and I want a new life after that? What if something happens to them? I can't believe I am making these ultra dark thoughts right now just to bring you to reason and only to splash you out your selfish bubble.

- Ok you are right. I am sorry. We have never discussed this and I assumed you are not bothered.

- I am clearly bothered! Menopause is like a first death. You are no longer young. Full stop. You can't even claim it. Full stop. And our bodies change. You can't ignore this agony even if you have 10 kids. Just get a grip babe!

- I am sorry. I have clearly upset you.

- It's not you I guess. I am angry at Mother Nature.

And I have not really processed this stage. No one talks about it. No one really prepares you for it. And we have only one another to support us. Or clearly not.

- She clearly did not like that last thing Anna gave Her. She is selfish or certainly self absorbed. She now realises Anna's point of how She thinks Bob the Manager evolves around Her or cares the slightest about who She is. She needs to start thinking outside Herself.

[*I will come to the rescue! I will use witty humour and sarcasm to take away the tension! Tell Anna:*]

- Well, Bob the Manager has us both covered. We have two lines on a policy to navigate this subject and support us.

- Yeah. I guess we have Bob... [*Anna's voice has clearly softened. My trick worked! Sarcasm for all difficult situations!*]

- But no really. I don't know. I guess we need to be open about these things. About the agony. Besides, it is not only about women. Everyone hates growing old and everyone is afraid to die in the end.

- Yes, but it gets too obvious with women. Too stressful. Too painful. And too soon. 40s??? It's the new 20s and it's not!

Yeah, you are right. Life at its best comes later

nowadays but you still need to chose a man and decide to have kids in the middle of it, just when you are not sure you have the skills to make choices. Because of menopause, there is less sobriety on women's part to chose a partner!

I know! All of sudden we turned 30 and the wedding invitations came flooding in. All these people met their important other the same year? Can't be true. It's just the clock ticking and the church bells are ringing.

This is a very difficult subject for a birthday morning in the office. Meet for a coffee at the usual place in 5'? Need a hug

I need a hug too. Meet you in 5'

Having a close friend close is a blessing. That is Her immediate thought. Anna's hug is exactly what She needs.

Would Mark's hug do the trick right now? He is bothered with age but he is not bothered with a terminal decision about kids, he has all the time in the world. So he will somehow only half understand Her? Should She not open up about this to Her man? [*Another clouded complicated thought today... The answer to your question is yes, by the way. We need to tell Mark our thoughts and fears*]

She is at the front of the cafe. Anna's delicate figure starts shaping in front Her. Some men's heads turn and it is clear Anna has this aura about her. You notice her. That kind of girl. A middle aged mother of 3, at the brick of no longer claiming to be young but you notice her. [*It could be that age is not the issue, right? It could be it's the attitude, right? And attitude is ageless. Better even, improves with age. I need to find something to control and hold on to today. Otherwise, feelings and most of all, fear of age will take over. I cannot allow that, I am your brain! You rely on me to keep you going. Right? Well yes, Brain, hold steady. I will, but please stop sabotaging!]*

Anna is now near Her. She wears this awesome blue dress, crop jacket, impressive artful jewelry. Smart but creative. Feminine but professional. [*Anna, is a very balanced person. One can tell by her style and she will then confirm with her behavior, life choices and reactions to things. I tend to believe now that a balanced soul demonstrates on choice of clothes and jewelry. A note for when we finally enroll in a master course in psychology and fashion after I have convinced us to leave conventional HR. I remember creating vivid images about this. Are they called dreams?*]

oh Anna - thank God you were available! I am really sorry for everything I said earlier

Well honey, I get it. You are worried about motherhood on top of ageing. I understand, fine. I did get angry but you have your point. It is such a disturbing issue.

Yeah I know. Younger it felt alright to overshare the tinniest detail about boyfriends and orgasms. With some sort of pride to it. Now that same body system is struggling but we don't feel safe to discuss about it.

Well Bob the Manager felt safe

Haha. Witty

We can discuss this with men and we don't dare to share with other women.

Well, I guess we want to pretend this is not happening

I guess. But, you know talking about it and feels like there is a shame to it.

Like the spinster guilt you mean? We fought so hard to shake off?

Yeah, I guess so. We are asked to spend our youth moulding ourselves to someone worthy of a good man and then? What happens then? There are the next stages and how have we prepared ourselves for them?

Yeah, like after marriage and kids, are you even worth living?

I read somewhere in fact that among mammals, only a few species carry on living after menopause!!

Are we being dramatic?

No Mother Nature is. And Mother Nature is also unfair.

I don't know. It could be the hormones

Hahaha

Can we talk about orgasms again please? And dating and mating and all that?

Sure, tell me about your last date with Steve. Did you meet in the kitchen or the corridor to the bathroom?

Haha. Both. We date a lot

Hahaha

Actually, I should ask Steve out on a date. Sometimes is not about growing old. Is about forgetting to live.

Steve is a great guy

I know. Bob the Manager is not

Well, yes. He gets selfish and shallow on occasion or procedural but he is not that bad. He caught the menopause wave. In his own way at least ...

Who else is a good apple there?

Outside Steve and Mark?

Yes, these two don't count

Well, wise Jim obviously

Wise Jim is a handsome, clever, super educated and kind man they have both known since college. They call him wise Jim because of his calm demeanor under any circumstances and his impressive emotional intelligence. He is not an artist by the way, which is superbly impressive. [*Well, he is not like an accountant or a hedge fund manager, either is he?* - Brain we are pigeon holing people here, no good. We work for HR! Unacceptable. - *Fine*]

Wise Jim is in fact a mathematician. And a skilled violinist for that matter. He has this patient, kind, welcoming personality. He goes about life minding his own business, not caring what other people think but deeply caring for other people. He knows his limits, respects the limits of others and has a sixth sense to call in when things are bad. [*I would not be surprised if he called right now, even though with the birthday that bet is not really crazy*].

He clearly had a crush for Her but back when things were possible. She thought he was not cool enough. Mark was and still is. Cool. So She is married to Mark. Mark is not always wise and Jim is. Back in the post college mating period wisdom was not a virtue. Now it seems like one but who can blame a young self for being young (and not wise).

She vividly brings to mind his kind face, with his blonde beard adding some masculinity to his otherwise baby face. He would still appear with the beard most of the time these days but it's color has arguably changed and so has Wise Jim: he does not care if people think he is baby face. He would rather embrace it and the confidence and wisdom in his eyes take away any thought of lack of masculinity. [*May I say that our handsome, well built, cool husband is childlike a bit too often and that takes away from his whatever machoness in seconds?* Fair point...]

In the next milliseconds before She goes back to Anna, the next thing that crosses her mind [*Why are we making these reference to a mind that is not me all of a sudden?*] is how likely it is that Wise Jim is excellent in bed... [*OK, seems like we are not anywhere near menopause here so false alarm ladies and gentlemen!*]

- I should call wise Jim and discuss this. Fresh perspective.

- I am sure he thinks like Steve. Steve and any man will be able to give offsprings whenever but aging is a concern, regardless. Besides, everybody wants to enjoy their kids, have them long in your life, play with them, see them grow. A kid in your 60s? You will hardly enjoy them when they can actually communicate properly and do fun things without risking killing themselves with just crossing a street. On top, you might want to have them with a woman who has a descent age difference to you and you are at the same wavelength in life. So Mother Nature and low AMH is not necessarily the blocker for him but pretty much he is on the same boat in the end.

- You have discussed this with Steve?

- Yes

- Really?

- We are a union of two people who share a house, a bed, a mortgage and our agonies you know?

For a moment there a sinking feeling came up. She has not had this conversation with Mark. Why? [*Are you measuring up Mark against other people now? Of course you do. Sorry I asked...Let's wrap this up. Bob the Manager, Mark, Steve, Wise Jim. It's getting crowded and confusing. Sip that flat white and go back to work*]

and what does Steve think? [*I was ignored once again... no matter the countless times this proved the wrong choice...*]

Well, he gets it how it is more obvious in women, and there is this terminability about it and he is very supportive. He has done some research to understand the situation slightly better.

The poor thing. I remember when you guys were expecting your first child. He would be in the library when he was not by your side talking to your bump!

Yeah I know. He is a bookie, I must admit. The thing is that he feels like ageing too, he has his own agonies about time and death. So no matter how different the demonstration of it feels, deep down we share the same problem

Yes, I see what you mean. He is not removing himself from it, claiming to be a woman's issue. He seems the we- are- all- mortals side of it.

Yes, something like that

Do you think he still fancies you?

Well, we are no longer on top of each other all day but I think he still sees the woman in me, on top of the mother, the old lady I am becoming or the one he just knows too well

That is so beautiful

Babe, we are still extremely young. You seem to jump ahead to our 50s and 60s. People start their lives at age 39 or a new love story for that matter. You need to stop obsessing with that number

I am so willing to agree but somehow, I am so stressed

[*We might in fact need Wise Jim here after all*]

You need your Mark to fuck the brains out of you tonight and then you will be back to normal!

[*I did not think of that and thought of Wise Jim?*]

I think I do!

Haha, not many anxiety problems sex cannot straighten out, right?

Not many, indeed

Babe, need to go.

Yes, of course. Same here, let's get back to work. Sorry I was harsh I guess. It's a very sad and disruptive one. Will call you later to say happy birthday. As due.

- Yeah, sorry I greyed your day. Speak later.

- Bye babe.

- Bye.

She heads back at her desk. [*Shall we call Jim?*] Dials Jim's number. Never presses the green button though. She stares at the little device in Her hand. She tries to make up Her mind. She is too immature and too naive to face what Wise Jim would say about Her agony and, at the same time, seems too immature to call Jim in the first place [*Well, we are not even 40 yet, ha! We can afford to be immature and naive and stupid! Press the green button hand!*]. She finds Her thoughts amusing. She will call him later, or he will call to wish happy birthday so the important thing is that they will get a chance to speak. [*Check a few lines above about being ignored and how wrong it has been...*]

She has this tendency to just tell people what bothers Her. Some think this is very selfish of Her. [*Anna just felt that, right? Calling her out of the blue and just throwing our agony at Her*]. Most people will usually remove themselves from Her once She has showered them with Her problems once or twice. She needs to be more sober, more careful [*Noted*].

She is now so perplexed, kind of sad and pessimistic She reached the stage She hopes in secret Her colleagues gather for a little happy birthday with all the shouting, the cake and the card with the boring wishes. She is actually looking forward to it when it seemed such an ordeal just moments ago. She really wants a nice cake right now. She has had a fair share of bitterness. She needs to balance it out. Swallow the sugar and fill the void [*We have repeatedly tried the fill-the-void-with-sugar method, have we not?? It only leads to weight gain which leads to an aggravated self-pity, that leads to depression, which makes it impossible to shake off the weight. The void is still there and no matter the layers of fat we put on top of it! I will switch off the dreaming of cake function immediately. Let me see. I have so many options. I will set us up to loathe broccoli and spinach instead. I need to take control here!*]

All of a sudden She has this funny crave for broccoli

and spinach. She shakes that off. Remembers the cake again. Feels better already [*This is sabotage!*]

She walks into the office. She notices Her office is actually nice. Maybe that compatible aesthetic has kept Her here so long. It's a nice location, natural light floods in, there are little corners to keep things interesting and the greatest thing of all there is art on the walls! She has been to those boring offices that are lines of desks under neon lights and the only thing on the wall is a company logo. Even worse, some company values no one values. They look so cheap, makes you feel cheap being there. The ones with the values reminds you of all the corporate lies. Imagine a couple not loving each other but keeping posts on the walls of their apartment with tag lines "There is only love in this place". If you need to be visually reminded to treat people with respect and professionalism, the collaboration and productivity ship has surely sailed...

She looks at the wonderful painting behind the boy at the front desk. It's as assembly of brushed color on a canvas. There is no theme jumping out of it but the colors are so well arranged and so generously offered to the starring eyes that can only make you smile. There was this idea some years ago when they moved into this office to support young artists. HR would go on galleries and schools to fetch some good but affordable art. The hope was that at least one of them would become the next Picasso and buy out all the investment by selling a single piece. Art has a very slow pace into fame so we are not there yet. She does enjoy that painting. It was not among the ones She picked but she had so much fun during the gallery trips. Made friends, met interesting people, free people, weird ones too. She needs more of that. She needs playfulness in Her life not just on Her wall. She does count Her blessings though. This is cheap art still but not frugal. This is a corporate office still but not a prison. [*What a big difference, a little color and a gentle thought can make...*]

She arrives at the desks area. She was right to guess there is a little happy birthday gathering with the smiles and the shouting. Someone even got a silly hat! Armed with the injection of love by Her friend and uplifting of color and gentle thoughts, She smiles at everyone and welcomes the little gathering with gratitude. HOWEVER, under some funny conspiracy of the universe, there is no cake. Just fruit! Vegan Dora is clearly to blame. She is not vegan. Dora is but that should be Dora's problem! She deserves Her cake. With sugar, butter and milk. And eggs! [*As a consolation, and let me remind you that broccoli and spinach at this point.... , let's agree it would have been ingredients you cannot pronounce and E705 this and E701 that, instead of just butter and eggs. You know, managing expectations and helping you face reality.* - Thanks Brain. Very pragmatic of you]

She sits on Her desk, fuming. She marks on Her to do list to slot a few lines on a policy, as requested by Bob the Manager. She is also thinking of coming up with a birthdays in the office policy, making mandatory to have CAKE! Still fuming, replies to a couple of emails and keeps Herself busy doing some research on female health issues, hormones and testaments on the men's perspective. She wants to do Her job well. She decided She will wait for people to call her. It's her birthday. Jim will surely will too. She is very curious of his perspective. She kind of missed him too.

She also makes the decision to go grab a muffin. It's her birthday. As this thought [*let's call it an excuse, shall we?*] rings in Her head, She feels happy. The sugar is nowhere near Her but just the thought of the muffin made Her Happy! [*a little pathetic, no? Let's blame our upbringing with all the chocolate and the sugary snacks around the house we grew up in. Things are better now…*]

She is already by the elevator. Door dings and no one seems to be in the cabin. She feels relieved. She makes it to the cafeteria at the ground floor in Her building. Finally! She has been flirting for quite some time with the thought to spending some money in this cafe since morning! It's a lovely coffee shop. Beyond the taste of the coffee itself, it is the people that make this cafe excellent! They know the regulars and spend some time chatting usually, if not too busy. She can see the girl at the counter offering a friendly smile as She walks in. It's that genuine smile not so much signaling how happy someone is but signaling the familiarity with Her existence. An acknowledgment She is there, She was there yesterday and the day before yesterday and all. It's a smile of continuity. Makes Her feel comfortable and seen. [*Let us not pretend we don't go there to check on the delicious man that usually makes our coffee too…*]

Hello, how are you today?

I am well. You?

Yes good. What can I get you?

Do you have any of your red velvet muffins?

In a cupcake?

Ah yes, I always confuse muffins and cupcakes.

I am afraid not but I can offer a slice of red velvet cake.

Yes, that is great. Pretty much same thing, if not better!

Yes mostly it is. I guess there would have been more frosting on the cupcake.

Fair point but I can settle

Fair enough. Coming

How come and you sold out so early?

The girl is delicately slicing a cake as she prepares to answer. There is a certain rhythm in how people who work in coffee shops move, She has noticed. They are slow, delicate and effective. As if there is a secret pact that coffee is a little of a ritual for everybody that cannot or should not be rushed.

Yeah, I do not know (she is now done cutting). I guess we are still a little hit and miss calculating our inventory now that people work from home a lot (the slice delicately finds itself in a cute box). I would say the conscious decision was to sell out early and run out than waste food too often.

I see. That makes sense. I would guess coffee shops scattered around corporate buildings were among the first to have to rethink ways of working, right?

Yes. The world changes all the time I guess. Here you are. (the cake in a cute box is lying there in front of her. Delicately wrapped up).

Thanks a lot.

That would be eight pounds please

Yes sure. Paying by card.

Of course.

She grabs the cake as if delicate and precious for some reason. Chips on the card machine and She is ready.

Thank you. Have a good day

You too.

She exits the shop. She is trying to think where best to enjoy Her cake. Weather seems alright outside. She takes a walk and swallows the cake indulgently as She walks. Her fingers get sticky and covered in frosting. Exactly like when She was kid. She thinks of nothing important for a while. It's just Her, the delicious cake and the city. Just like when She was a kid.

CHAPTER THE ONE CLOSEST TO THE HEART FRIEND WITH A SURPRISE

She takes a few deep breathes. Quite a few childhood memories popped in her head. Anna is on most of them. Making them good.

Makes Her way upstairs and back at Her desk. She has spent quite some time away from Her desk now, feels She needs to go back. Makes no sense to waste a day at work. If that is what She will end up doing, better to have called in sick and really enjoy the day. Ghosting it off doing neither work nor anything really fun makes no sense.

She is going through emails for a while. She is in admin mode and no matter how hard She tries to talk Herself into productivity, can't fathom the energy to do any serious work. Goes around offices and chats, people reach out happily to wish Her happy birthday. There is gossip for the choice of fruit as birthday treat and whether it's a good idea to repeat that. She has not confirmed with many that She ate the muffin to console herself. [*That would have cemented the fruit gossip though.* - That would be too much information Brain. Unnecessary drama]

She does not really like office gossip anyway so She would not care to fuel it with the "I craved a muffin [*cupcake woman!*] confession. She also strongly believes it's part of Her job to stay away from gossip, being HR. However, honestly, She has never come across any worse gossipers than HR colleagues. Somehow knowing salaries and dirt about people is tempting information to share? Too much power to handle? Too much information to compare one's circumstances against?

She has all these principles and ideas what the function should be and She is trying to make as much of it a reality as possible. Like push for the best of employees, be by their side, support them on a path to maturity, well being and productivity. Happiness and fulfillment really.

Bob the Manager has been an impediment. He sees HR as a corporate thing. Something upper management needs in order to control people. He likes the management part of the job, not the human. Human MANAGEMENT. Bob the Manager would rather lead with fear, if lead at all. He only cares for himself really. Kind of hard to believe he has anything to do with humans. Or maybe that is it. He sees humans really as resources. Means to and end. So he leads the Human Resources function...

In any event, even if She started making corporate a better place by fighting office gossip, She cannot uproot from people's hearts how misery likes company. That is what gossip stems from. Humans like to talk about things as if talking it out loud will make it go away.

She got lost in thoughts for a while. She can tell She feels tired. Checks on the bottom right of Her screen. 4.50pm it says. She can't believe the office day is over! Said a few more thank yous as people mentioned the birthday occasion. No one asked Her age. Kindness? Political correctness? Too obviously old to make it tactful to ask? Felt good She did not have to answer "39" and deal with the comments that would have come with it. Thanks society for tact and political correctness!

She is out in the open air. Feels better. She is waiting to meet Her friend for a little shopping. She spots a man. Late 50s, average built, kind of good looking. Smart jacket, well groomed. He seems interested to start a conversation. He is playing with a cigarette, possibly have not made up his mind whether to light it or not. He seems bored. Looking Her way and smiling, not in the flirtatious but in the oh-another-human-being way. She still feels something tingling (random conversations on the street have stop happening as often as they used to). Tinder and online dating have definitely taken their toll to spontaneous flirting but then again, maybe it's just age. This time She does not mean it in a deteriorating way. She knows She can be interesting for a man. It's more about the attitude. The serious posture, the "I have too much on my mind posture" and the likelihood She is someone's wife or mother already which might discourage suitors... Or, in all honesty, it might just be the wrinkles.

She spent too much time on Her thoughts. The not bad at all late 50s guy is gone? She had not even met him and made so many assumptions about him! She has the weird feeling he became important. She was so flattered in the thought a man might be interested in flirting with Her or at least spark a conversation and now he is gone and She feels disappointed! [*That is insane. We can't be that depressed and desperate.*]

Hi

(The man is just standing there. He never left. What is wrong with Her?) Hi

I can't stop noticing the badge on your jacket so happy birthday I guess

(The girls at the office had given Her a silly hat and other paraphernalia with the tag Birthday Girl all over) Ah yes, forgot to remove that. Thank you. I am indeed quite obviously the birthday girl

yeah

Yes, girls in the office got excited.

Men tend not to do this silly demonstration. It's a beer and happy birthday mate

[*Is he comparing men to women now? Are we getting into the women are from Venus and men from Mars zone?*] Yes, a little more sober in demonstration but not in the literal sense (She kind of felt competitive there. She is actually proud of Her line)

Spot on. How many pink candles on the cake then?

[*He missed the political correctness memo? Did he*

just asked us our age quite bluntly?] 39 (people tend to be extremely honest and brave with strangers)

Oh, 39. Tough

(She resorts to a smile. She feels weird. Moments ago this man was even getting important. Now She wishes Her friend is on time if not early) Why tough?

Oh I am sure you know what I mean. For a woman the clock is ticking. You run out of time any time soon. But I am getting ahead of myself, you probably have kids and a husband and you can't be bothered with anything else than school runs, school meals and a mums' whats app group

I am not sure I understand. No I don't have kids

Well then, no matter how sober you want to sound, I am sure 39 gave you a good degree of panic

[-Brain, have you been talking to this gentleman all day? He seems too informed or too alike to all the silly thoughts and comments you have been giving me! *I was not the one with the silly thoughts...*] Why should it? (She is really trying to be sober. He is right. She has been panicking. Then again, isn't he kind of audacious if not obnoxious? Can he really talk like that? Is it legal these days?)

I feel I am wasting time stating the obvious here. A woman past her prime with no kids. Soon aging will accelerate as you get to menopause and everything important in a woman is taken away. You live all your lives as beautiful dolls dying to become mothers and then it's over I guess. It even gets harder to get a job without the charm of freshness

(She is angry now. He is just a stranger. She can be rude. She can pick up a fight. That will surely make Her feel better for the first 2' or two hours - depending how far She goes, 2 days. She is calculating. Probably worth it! Changes Her mind. She can't waste 2' from Her precious [and arguably thinning] time on planet Earth on this creature with a lizard brain) I think you are right, very accurate and enlightening observations [We are so proud! Cynicism, we love it!]

(He resorts to a smile)

(She turns the other way. Checking her phone - savior in any awkward social moment for sure). They never speak again

They do however stand close to each other. Worlds apart but physically close. Or worlds apart consciously but somehow connected through Her fear. Her fear connects to him still. She feels as if She is not removed from that conversation. As if it has not ended. They don't speak. They will never speak again. They will never meet again. However, this man has become a part of Her now. She will remember him for a while. This is insane but true! He tapped into Her fear so deeply that She will speak about him. Think about this conversation. She is not calm, because of him. This is a profound impact on Her from a total stranger. This is what fear can do to Her.

[I wonder, did we have any impact on him? What made

him talk to us? What made him so audacious? Did we somehow invite this? Did he sort of "smell" our fear, our thoughts? It is genuinely bizarre that he went straight into that subject with no tact, no remorse. Will he ever think he may have insulted or wounded a stranger? Does he even have the power to do that? Or our fear did?]

She tries to shake off all these thoughts. [- Brain, thank you but your observations are not helping me now. That psychology degree never happened. I am just in HR. Deal with it!]

She tries to shake him off. She has not registered much of his figure thank God! She will soon not remember his voice either. It's up to Her to forget about him altogether. Leave no room for him.

[• Right Brain? Did you roger that???]

She has not bothered to notice what happened to him. Lost in Her thoughts and stressed to shake him off, She did not turn towards him a single time. She even blocked Her peripheral vision [technically that was me blocking the vision you wanted to block btw, just for the record. I did roger. Thank you]

Had She bothered or not had been too scared to even gaze at his direction She would have noticed a 22year old blonde carrying bags from expensive stores coming to meet him. No one can tell. Could be a daughter or relative. In some countries relatives kiss on the lips...

Jess is here. Not late but She thinks it took her for ever.

Hi birthday girl!!!

Jess is a fun, complicated, honest, clever, creative, wonderful creature She absolutely admires, loves and trusts. They met at a random corporate event when Jess was still in corporate. They started talking and soon laughing and have not stopped since. There have been less joyful moments obviously but their hearts bonded and have been close with no disruptions. She is one of those friends that match Her best version of Herself. She mirrors on Jess anything that is good in Her. It feels great. That mirror also helps Her get even better, grow. Reminds Her how good it feels to love and be loved.

Hello!

Hey, are you upset or something?

oh no. Not really.

You were not very excited to see me

haha. I am relieved and happy to see you, you cannot imagine

Are you surely alright? Birthdays are funny days

No I am fine. I only had a weird encounter with a stranger so got a little affected

What happened?

Well, not worth our time. Just a guy in late 50s. Spotted my badge (brings her hand to her coat to take it out as She remembers it's there still) and said happy birthday. Asked my age and then started a harangue on women being past their prime and worthless

No way?

He did

No!

I am telling you

Isn't that illegal these days? Let's find an officer!

Hahaha - you are so funny. Well, apparently not. Had it been illegal to be a jerk there would not be enough room in prisons

True

Well, the poor guy is having his own middle life crisis, what do you care?

(She just realized the man was probably in his own agony indeed. Who on their right minds would think like that and have the nerve to discuss it. *It's called mirroring*. Her brain picking up random knowledge again. Her Brain has not given up and still makes the case for that psychology degree) I had not thought of that. I got consumed in my own agony

What agony?

Well, he hit me on my soft spot. I have been depressed since I woke up. I don't like being 39. I want to stick to 30. Nothing to change, nothing to move from there.

Honey, too late. You have already moved.

I know, but it sucks. It seems like I didn't know what I was doing when I was at my prime, wasted it all instead of investing it and here I am miserable, failed and old. And will only get worse. I will get older and even more depressed and my chances and tools and the time to put my life on track will vanish

Ok. That is a little too much.

Jess I know you will start telling me all the optimistic stuff people say on this occasion and I would say all these stuff to you if it was your birthday and your crisis but I am afraid it's true

Ok. Let's be depressed and desperate then. I signed up to come and meet you for a girly afternoon shopping. Can I get my money back?

You are so funny.

I am 41 my love. I have a good sense of humor because I am getting wise. You can tell I have a good sense of humor because you are getting wise too. You are admittedly a little left behind though. What sort of non sensical self talk is that?

Hello darkness my old friend

Well, you can go shopping with your friend Ms darkness and when she is out come and meet me for girly drinks?

Ok fine. I may just need a hug than a lecture

Did I even lecture you? You know how it feels if I start

Ok, not the real thing but on the verge of

Ok you need a hug. And a gorgeous dress and sexy underwear all wrapped in some nice shopping bag. And a martini?

Lucky me

It's your birthday. Queen of the day. Queen of drama you may be too

(Jess spreads her arms and She nestles in like a kid)

But I mean, even if your jokes take the drama away, menopause is really ante portes

Oh Lord, you are really into this

It is on my mind all day

That is the most interesting choice of subject for a birthday. Menopause. Let's discuss menopause.

Great! Let's openly discuss menopause. Share the agony. How often do you think about it?

Can we move a bit? I am such an old lady cannot get depressed standing you know. I need to move or a drink

She smiles. Fair enough

So, how often is it on your mind?

I don't know honey. Did you think about it before it was birthday today?

You know, ever since my first cycle, I have been getting stressed once a month. Will it happen? When will it happen? What will it look like? Am I pregnant? And now this new agony: am I perimenopausal?

I get that. It is a thing on my mind once a month too. I would not say I am equally consciously stressed about it if I am not worried about something specifically, but it is there, I agree

For me it's like a reminder at minimum. A clock that says an end is near. I want to lose track of time and I can't!

I have never thought about it like that, but I see what you say. I guess more women out there can feel like that.

I am surprised you are sober about it

I am not sober, I just took for granted for that part of my life and have not been thinking about it that much every month. I kind of assume it is going to be there and looking alright. Why agonise?

Possibly a very healthy approach to it.

Why agonise and not a take a test honey? Check where you are. Perhaps you can calculate how near or afar you are to this whole peri or actual menopause. You are fairly young and why agonise over something that has not happened yet?

I don't know. This birthday gets me. I don't want to grow old

Ok, you have some soul digging to do. You need to come to terms with life.

Ha! As if that was simple

It is not. But the sooner you come to terms with reality the better

Like you are in terms with reality?

Not all of it. But I try to save what I agonise over

Sensible.

Why are we talking about menopause and not babies though? What are you guys doing? With Mark I mean

I don't know. I guess we are lazy or coward or both and will end up empty nesters and regret it?

That is a very sensible and mature way to address the question

You are being judgmental for a second there lady

Guilty as charged. I am not perfect

How about you? You had mentioned you wanted a child but Sam was against it?

Not against it, just lazy and coward I guess (they both start laughing)

Life is just wonderful without kids, right?

I don't know. Only moments ago you said your life was a wasted line of years and a failure. Please chose

Hahaha, well better to fail and face the music alone

You are lazy and coward or what. And I am proudly judgmental here

I guess I need to take things seriously.

Exactly. I guess you agonise about something that has not happened yet to avoid making a choice over something tangible and urgent?

We seem to be looking into my soul...

You gave me the keys, years ago

I hate this urgency!

Well, you could have had your kids in your late 20s and early 30s as everybody else you know. Now you would not feel the urgency

That is not fair still Jess! Men live their modern lives and they do not even think about it. When they want one they go for it. They don't calculate years. They don't fit a baby into their career lines only because they are 30. They might even chose partners more relaxed and sober in the end cause they can afford to wait

you think so?

Totally!

How are things with Mark sweetie? I am a little concerned hearing you saying all this

No everything is fine. I think I am just in a middle life crisis

Well, to be fair to men, they do go through a middle life crisis

Yes. I guess. How are things with you? How are things with Sam?

Sam does not seem to care about babies at all. Either because she is 30, or she genuinely made up her mind not to care or she is lazy and coward. Have been suggesting that I want to experience motherhood and she has been dismissive rather. Like my problem not hers. It feels like even if I was magically pregnant tomorrow she would stay out of the whole kid agenda and she will get only the coupling out of us. And I guess leave when bored

But do you want to experience motherhood or experience you and Sam becoming a family?

Spot on comment there. Not sure. I know I want to experience motherhood but can you really be a family if the 50% is indifferent?

Is she indifferent or scared?

Well she has this painful divorce and terrible things happening in her past and in her wider family. An analyst might say she is scared. I can only believe what she is telling me, though

Tricky.

I know. I actually did a blood test. I found this kit that you can order online and they give you your egg count and all so that you make informed decisions. You should do it too. It will help you stay informed rather than blindly scared and panicking

I heard about that. Anna suggested I do it. I should do it. What was your report?

Not terribly optimistic. I should hurry if I want kids naturally. I knew the test would not come out extremely optimistic. Mum and aunt were done with menopause by age forty five.

I am sorry to hear that. I mean your agony (She realises She has been consumed with herself. [*Didn't we do that with Anna just a while ago? What are we turning into?*] The women closest to her heart go through agonies similar to Hers. If not more complicated. That is somehow both sad but also reassuring. Common human, woman experience. Should be shared)

I am glad you brought it up actually. Let's sip some bubbles cheering the stranger on the street who inflicted his middle life crisis on you! And now us

Ha, let's do that. He would not have menopause though

Seems like they get the trouble though. And it might be more of a shock to them actually, as they were never tracking time bleeding like a clockwork every month, they might get a shock when they realise the time is up

to middle life crisis then!

off we go

They did go for the shopping. The sexy dress and the lingerie. Laughed it all out and ended in that amazing cocktail bar sipping some bubbles, talking menopause and babies at the same time. Jess was making so much fun at the lingerie department wondering if lace makes any sense for perimenopausal 40 year olds. Jess is just wonderful. Not sexy nor attractive in any traditional sense but charming with her wit and sense of humor. Definitely very brainy. She realised Jess gave Her away her secret: come to terms with reality. And the sooner, the better.

They spent a couple of hours together and She feels lift up. Wondering if Jess on the other hand feels dragged down. Is She toxic and selfish? [*Woman, any other negative self talk today? I am getting miserable!*]

She really needs to go through this day and tomorrow She will be Her old sober and capable self. Maybe just welcoming all these thoughts and allowing Herself to be scared and in agony is the best She can do. She cannot just walk around inflicting middle life crisis to people. She needs to do some soul searching indeed and maybe talk it all out with Mark. What are they doing with the baby after all? Why has She allowed the uncertainty over this? Thinks of wise Steve again for a second. Weird.

CHAPTER THE MOTHER

She clinks on Her shopping bags. Mark will have his jaw dropping for sure. She will look devine tonight. That is a better thought for the day than all the middle life crisis ones. One more stop before She heads home though. A quick visit to Mum's. For some reason, all Her life, She is the one with the duty to visit Mum. She suddenly realises it would have been normal to expect Mum to take care of Her at least on Her birthday. She should feel obliged of nothing. [*What would really happen if we go straight home? What if we care for us and not for Mum for a change? It is a convoluted situation for the daughter to act like the love provider... Just saying -* I don't have the energy for a revolution right now. I promise I will consider it next time *- Whatever...*]

Mum has been taking care of grandma and they now live together. Surely though, grandma is still taking care of Mum. At least emotionally. So everybody is taking care of Mum and Mum is alleviated from all expectations [*Mum is going places, or what?*] She thinks that Dad was doing the same. Her Dad, Her kind, strong, wise superhuman Dad died when She was 30. Heart attack. Her heart, it was Her heart attacked. And broken. She misses him. Mum is not fun. Competitive and immature and complex and selfish. Still wonders why on earth these two were together.

She knows the story. Dad was just walking by grandma's house and saw Mum in the garden. He immediately fell in love with her. She was and still is admittedly very beautiful. Dad moved mountains to convince Mum to be with him. Maybe it was a sense of bet, some sort of lack of confidence of his that he fed by marrying La Belle. Who knows. He had been trying hard to keep her happy throughout their lives. Mum always in tantrums asking for more and more, never grateful enough, never cool enough. She somehow gets sad thinking of Her parents. She loved Dad. He was fun and always tried to solve problems. Problems that did not really exist and only Mum would create and inflict on him. Still, though, he seemed not to mind. He carried through life with a smile. She guesses deep down he was troubled, hence the heart failure. He was hiding things in his heart so it popped one day.

It usually proves disappointing to spend time with Her Mum. She will stick to tradition and drop by regardless. Mum will have made a cake (she is a good baker) but nothing more and she will start asking questions about Mark and grandchildren. She has been playing along all Her life. Pretending Mum is good and treating Her with love as she lacks the nerve to really say how She feels. [*Possibly what Dad was doing?*]

The honest thing is She feels neglected. It's never about Her. It's always about Her mum. Always. Ever since She was a child She was forced into putting on a show to keep Mum calm and happy. If She did anything authentic, or claimed any real attention or mentioned She had needs, the Hell would brake lose. An endless blame game would begin, with Her feeling hurt and misunderstood and alone. She is used to the show now. She thinks fighting the fight is pointless. Her mum will not change and She will come out of it exhausted and cancelled. [*Is this really the only outcome? We do realise we are no longer five years old, right? We are not obliged to play the show. We are not obliged to drop by mum's. We can tell her she is a bitch. Just want to make sure we understand the the options here. I could not guide you when we were five properly, but birthdays do come with maturity. Maturity = realising you have options. Felt compelled to clarify.* - well thanks Brain. Let's see what you can really do now that we are 39 and not 5! *Like you are ready for the challenge Dear?*]

Hello! Birthday girl is home!

Surprise!!!

A random selection of grandma's friends from her card game and a bunch of neighbors are all cheerfully screaming happy birthday at Her the moment She opens the door.

[*Honestly, who are these people and how did they know we are coming and what time?*

- *No idea Brain. I was getting all adult prep to face Mum but this is not expected. Need time*]

She scans the room for Mum. Mum sits somewhere by the side. She cannot tell if Mum invited this, accepted it or reprimands it. Poker face Mum at its best.

She has always had this trouble with Mum. Mum would

not give away the slightest of feelings but rage. Oh lord, if Mum was angry the world would know and the world would burn! She developed the perfect skill of becoming invisible. The perfect skill of patiently waiting for the outburst to calm down. Perfectly believing She was to blame for the outburst. [*I do admit that back when we were five the thought that made the more sense for me to give you is that because you played with toys and laughed loudly she became angry. Sorry, this is how I could work through correlations back then. I know different now.*

• *Sure, but what can we do to fix it dear Brain?*]

The neighbors and friends must have been in the house for a while. They seem impatient for the cake. She scans the room more carefully and She can see the pile of dishes and pizza boxes as a justification for their impatience.

She is genuinely surprised all these people are there. She can understand this has more to do with Grandma than Her. Still, She feels like a birthday girl. And most importantly She feels like a girl. A little girl with a team of people around Her to care for Her and protect Her. That warms up Her heart.

Hey my beautiful child! Happy birthday. Grandma gives her a huge, strong hug despite her age. She hugs back, tenderly and caringly. Grandma is 82. If She stressed about 39 how would 79 feel? [*Possibly 89 feels great, though, right? Possibly Brain*]

The friends and the neighbors are all giving Her nice wishes and smiles. It's so not the case any more that neighbors would pop by on a short notice to be part of a family event. She realises She has no idea who Her neighbors are. [*Besides, they change all the time. How bonded can you feel with a 12months tenant? Or how invested do you care to be when you are the 12months tenant?* - Thank you Brain that was a very elaborate and balanced analysis of modern real estate and its impact on social norms...

   - Pleasure]

Mum gives Her a hug and a kiss. Mum is like always out of place. Always like she is pretending to be a mum. As if she is lost in her role, unsure or unwilling to play it even. She has been managing by copying other mums, real ones or from movies. Mum does not know Her needs nor Her habits. Mum just plays a part. Mum is always stressed as a result of that. It's normal to be stressed when you put on a show. You are waiting for some reward. She feels like Mum is constantly in the middle of a test. A test she has put on herself and secretly hoping she will fail and drop trying. She really, really desperately hopes Her mum turns into a genuine human who at some point gave birth to another human. She would give anything to make that show stop. Now. [*Just do it! I stole that line from a popular shoe retailer admittedly but that is exactly what I need you to hear right now!]*

One of the neighbors-guests helps Her tune back into the little party grandma has going on.

So, how is Mark? Still together?

(She definitely expected this question - with another

choice of words obviously - from Mum. Not this woman. And what on earth does she mean, "still together?" Like, why would they not be together? Is someone fixing bets on the duration of Her marriage behind Her back? What do they know? What do they sense? What is She not admitting?)

Yeah he is fine, thanks (she leaves the second question purposefully unanswered. Or maybe She does not know the answer...)

Good. Good. Excellent

Work? (Who is this woman and why is she on a mission to get on Her nerves. Rather uncivil questions on a birthday. She takes a mental note to find a local governor and make it illegal to ask questions like these. Especially on a birthday. [*The legal system is very disappointing, isn't it?* Not now brain! This is not the time to dwell off sociological analysis of the impact of the law. Be busy finding a clever way to get away from this woman!]

Yeah all good, let me just pop in the loo for a second. I have not had a chance to settle with this beautiful surprise going on [- Brain, really???]

The party, the awkward questioning, the jokes that have nothing to do with Her carry on for a while. Of grandma's neighbors those who live the closest will stay for a little longer for sure. She will need to make a move soon and head home. It's getting late. The cake was awesome. She tells Mum. She confidently smiles back and offers to wrap it up and they can finish it off with Mark.

She kisses Mum. She can see she is getting old too. She senses how she needs to be taken care of but Grandma is too old now, She is too unwilling and Mum will push anyone else away. Maybe grandma was always too self sufficient, too self absorbed for Mum. With her social connections, her parties, her extroversion. Maybe Mum has been lonely and neglected all her life. Possibly very happy with the loving, caring, generous man Dad was. She now settles for whatever Grandma can offer, and it was never much? [*Turning empathetic there Mrs 39? - Yes, Brain, I may finally start to understand the person behind my Mum. - Yes possibly she might have been a sub parr mum but she is still a person indeed*].

Mum, do you want to go out next week? The two of us? (She is not sure where that came from. She is not even sure it is a good idea. [*Exactly. I had nothing to do with it! Just another one of your impulses*] It is very probable the night will be a disaster. They will end up fighting and despising each other, as ever. Is she in denial about Mum? [*Well, we cannot end up fighting with Mum unless we chose to, you know. -Thanks Brain, it takes two to tango, ok, but to who picks the tune? Don't be immature please... - Are you being judgmental Brain?*]

Honey, are you OK? (Of course Mum picks this up as a sign She is not not Ok. She can't see what She is suggesting)

I am asking to spend some quality time with you (She would normally add "what is wrong with you". She decides not to this time. It took two heavy breaths but She did it)

This little party did not give us a chance to chat, you know. Connect

Oh honey. Yes sure

I miss you (She means I miss the Mum you should have been but She will play with what She has. They are all getting too old to carry on with their passive aggressive patterns and failed chances to love)

Oh my baby. (Mum is genuinely touched. Mum hugs Her. Mum's hug feels like a thank you. She is not sure what can of worms She opened. Maybe it's just a door. To be seen. Next week. The dinner might never happen anyhow. Mum tends to be passive with these things. She will think it off later)

Need to head home.

(She would normally say "Love you" now. Without meaning exactly that. Now She is full with feelings and Her heart feels warm and full. She needs to find different words to express that as "Love you" has long lost its meaning and deteriorated into "Bye now". She needs to reinvent language.. or love.)

She checks on Grandma. She is once again overdressed for the occasion. A long blue dress, excessive jewelry on her neck [*is that feathers??*]. She has always managed to look a diva and never ridiculous somehow. The same outfit on anyone else would have crossed that fine line a lot easier. She remembers Grandma would always be full of joy and beaming in social events but her delicate clothes would act like a barrier to real touch, to real connection. Could never really hug grandma or sit on her laps for too long. The cresses would appear on her fashionable outfit and that she would not forgive. Was that Grandma's trick? You can look but cannot touch. Who and what was she hiding in those deux pieces and divine dresses?

She would have loved to just have them both sit down in front of Her and question them about going old. How menopause was to them, how motherhood was to them, how losing their man was to them. How going through life feels. She needs guidance and support and wisdom. She got small talk and cake. Again.

Lovely little surprise there Grandma. Thanks for the party

Could not resist it dear. It's my little granddaughter's big birthday

I can imagine. It was fun thanks

Glad you liked it

Your friends are sticking around?

Yes, the ones living close by will stick around for a card game or something

Win big Grandma!

Will do! You bring me luck

Sure. I am off, I will check in again next time

Ciao dear

Bye (kisses Grandma and turns back to leave).

It has only just occurred to Her, that Grandma did not ask Her anything. She put on the show and the surprise for herself. An excuse to bring people home and have fun herself? She did not ask Her anything. Anything at all. She is just absorbed by her little party. She only just realised that Mum has been lonely indeed. Maybe she is not the Mum She needs because she had no role model. Maybe she is stuck into the frustrated daughter situation, or Mum is still just hungry for love herself so she cannot give any. She has nothing in the tank, her tank was never filled. She leaves the house with a sense of sudden clarity, huge empathy and the strength to finally understand the person behind the Mum. She needs to think about forgiving still. She is not sure understanding is enough.

On her way home She books a consultation with a fertility expert. She will surely have to go through a million blood tests. AMH this and scan the other. She feels best to know how close She is to youth or death [*a little dramatic there?? - That is how I feel Brain! - Oh boy, feelings against reason again...*] Mark does not have to know [*Well, my immediate thought now is that Anna would have told Steve. Before making the call. Just saying*]

She suddenly feels in control of her destiny. That false sense that She is doing something about something She absolutely cannot control [*I am the voice of reason, I live in your head and I cannot even control this urge to pretend we control life. Maybe I created these dysfunctional stress coping, in fact, but can we please forget it? - Too late Brain. I love your coping mechanisms now!*]

CHAPTER BACK HOME

She can't wait to throw Her office clothes away and hop into the shower. Throughout Her work life, this has been a vital routine. If She could, She would burn those office clothes every day and step into the hottest bath tab for an hour. Lack of finances and fear of scalding makes Her settle for laundry and a warm shower. She feels She can't get rid of the office mood otherwise. She has done all these different things with all these different people after the office, yet She has this urgent need to change. Her showers are like a water curtain: She switches to professional mode taking a shower in the morning before work and then She switches to Her good old self in the afternoon taking that after work shower. Sometimes She uses the gym as that switch [*which hello! Also involves a shower*]. Water bill and expensive shower gels with different aromas is the price She is willing to pay to keep Her true self unpolluted from Her office avatar.

She wraps herself with the bathrobe and feels like a sexy birthday girl already. She had a pedicure the other day and Her shopping spree yielded that amazing lingerie set. She is a "girl with a plan" as the clever girl that attended to Her at the lingerie shop commented.

She can't understand why all that menopause hysteria enveloped Her all day. She is not a spinster after all. She has Mark. And a plan. The clock is ticking and it's about time they move on now. She feels ready to step into a new chapter in life. She has been this "young adult" enjoying life, travelling, shopping and just spending money because She is independent and carefree as would be the nice way to put it. Cocktails and golden beaches all look alike in the recent years though. She has spent a good amount of time in that chapter of life. She needs to move on. Experience another bit of life.

She is 39. She needs to become a mum. She must become a mum. [*hmm, wait a minute. A lot of musts and shoulds there. Do we want to become a mum?*] She surely has no time to waste. It's either mum or menopause. Young adult does not seem like something that will be on the cards for long.

[*Are we sure about this? Is Mark the one? Is a ticking clock enough to get us into motherhood? Ok young adult might be a little of a definition to stretch but, just adult should be OK, no?* - Brain, enough. Everybody has kids and I will too. And it's now or never kind of. - *Shouldn't we get the data first? We booked a visit to the doctor earlier, didn't we?* - We will. But tonight is a birthday night. Birthday sex is a given. Unprotected birthday sex it will be! - *We seem determined, but does not feel mature and safe. I have been consistently ignored when it comes to boys. Historically....*]

Mark seems to have been onboard but somehow reluctantly. Her friends say he is just scared of growing up, She feels it is something deeper but it could be Her insecurity talking. Right? [Brain?? Now is the time to say something as a consolation pleeeeaaase. - *Nope. No matter what I say, the rest of this body does whatever it likes when it comes to men! I will not labour for no cause. I will start reminding us of songs and do nothing useful!*]

Shakes that thought off. The body lotion sensual aroma helped. Jesus, what do they put in these things?! The lotion has a slight glimmer. She looks herself in the mirror. She smiles. Gym and genes have done their job, a little diet is needed.

Hair. Nothing changed since this morning really. Hard to tame as always...

She gets ready. Mark will be home soon. She does not want to have a sneak pick at the fridge and check what he has been preparing. She wants the surprise. She likes surprises. [*Something in common with Grandma?*]

Ready. Lights up that ridiculously expensive candle She has been saving for special occasions. Pops Herself a glass of red wine, puts on Her favorite playlist, melts on Her sofa, closes Her eyes, waits for Mark, dreams of that next chapter in life. 39. She must have time. Well, panic and misery can wait. Mark will be home soon. His hug, his touch will be home soon too. Smiles happily.

Mark is that classic I can get crazy for you kind of guy. Well built, six foot tall, good looking. His set of green eyes are full of meaning, they carry a piercing message. He takes care of himself, dresses well, goes to the gym, knows his wine, cooks exceptionally. He likes to travel, he likes to party. People around him feel fun and they get some. He is popular at work, popular among his friends. Constantly flirtatious [*now is that a good thing???*] and up for some adventure. The I can get crazy for you guy.

And that is what She did. She was crazy for him. Their dating phase was so exciting. So full of fun, travel, sex. Repeat. They were young, electrified by each other, with good prospects in life. They met at the right age, the right way, they had the right jobs, they could afford the right flat, they felt right for each other. He proposed. She said yes. They had the right wedding. She wore the right dress. They looked so right on the pictures afterwards.

She is in fact looking at one of their wedding photos right now. It's on the furniture in front of Her, with that well arranged bouquet by it. She replaces that bouquet ever so often. It's kind of the first thing to look at when entering the flat. Memories for the wedding flood Her head. She likes looking at pictures. She has them spread around the house. Such an old school thing to do. She likes this arrangement. As a kid She would go around Grandma's and the pictures were everywhere. Back then, scattering framed pictures around was the closest people would get to insta stories to remind or convince themselves of the good times. [*Humanity does not progress, only technology does*].

She mentally goes through moments with Mark. He was really gorgeous at the wedding. So confident in his suite. Surrounded by his best friends who just kept playing jokes at him. He looked at Her when She appeared at the aisle and said nothing but his eyes were filled with a combination of admiration, lust and love. [*It's been a while since we last saw that gaze, no?*]

She remembers the honeymoon afterwards and all

the travelling they have done together. Europe, Asia... Summers in the Mediterranean, winters in Kentucky and NY. She always wanted to travel on Her birthday. What happened this year? Is She really getting old after all? And rusty? Anyway, growing old with someone is so unique. Kind of scary and comforting alike. She likes that thought. Closes Her eyes and gets carried away down memory lane.

Turnkey sound at the door. Some whooshing comes with it. [*we did not expect that!*]

"Oh thank God you are home and not naked"!! For a moment we thought you would be laying around like Julia Roberts in pretty woman after her shopping spree. But then, this is your birthday and not Mark's so we felt more comfortable" Hahahaha - Oh HAPPY BIRTHDAY!!"

[*WTF???*]

She is attacked by a hug that follows this slightly incomprehensible, loud, unexpected [*unwelcome? - yes, thank you Brain*] outburst of love (?) from this semi drunk woman She identifies, when the initial shock subsides, as one of their friends.

By the way, there is a clear distinction in Her head between Her friends, their friends and Mark's friends. For some reason Her friends and their partners did not all become their friends or not fully. But all his friends and their partners have... She is more tolerant, or more of a full or less capable of boundaries and assertiveness?

She can see Mark. He is semi drunk too. Clearly. There

is the casualness, the messed hair, the cresses on the clothes. The clear signs. This state though makes him look even more gorgeous. [*We were clearly in another mood before that turnkey obviously. So it will take some time to forget thinking of wild unprotected sex, which was the case just seconds ago*]

No matter how gorgeous he seems and how horny of a state She has been in, there is now confusion, disappointment, surprise, nervousness and curiosity what this is all about. Who are these people invading Her home on this day? Why is Mark not Hers alone today? Why is he drunk? Or tipsy at least. Why are uninvited people storming into Her night? She should have had a saying to all this. Ok a moment ago She was saying She likes surprises and, Dear Universe, even though you rarely listen after all, this is what you understood?

She quickly calculates She'd better turn on "social, happy face mode" and forget about what She was dreaming seconds ago. Is this really about Her? Is this relevant, appropriate even on a birthday? Is She grumpy and ungrateful and inhospitable?

[*Am I expected to cope with all these questions?*]

Mark kisses her. Bad breath obviously. [*Feels a little procedural? Look, we are kind of messed up now. Happy, social face though has endured through much worse. We can do this!*]

Hello everyone!! Did you start a party without me someplace? [*This is our flat. We can kick them all out. Well, maybe not Mark, technically his flat too. - Brain, you* are right and not. Switch to happy mood and keep it on until instructed otherwise].

Their friend and Mark are all so happy and laughing and swooping around the flat, making themselves comfortable and well into making a little party out of this.

-Adeola, Jean and Marcella will be coming over too. Possibly, Hector from work too. He fancies Adeola and it's about time they get a chance. Right babe? [... *Brain! On until instructed. Please*]

Yes that is nice. A little match making will spice it all up

Don't worry about food. Nor wine. I have everything covered. I have cake covered too. Obviously.

[*Can I turn passive aggressive mode on? Or happy is what we stick to?* - Happy. Until instructed]

Oh sweetie. That is lovely.

She wants to break off happy, social mood and get him into the corner of the kitchen and get Her answers. Why on earth and in his sound mind did he chose to bring all these people over? On Her birthday? This is not even a surprise party. It's just a bunch of people he wants to meet? He could have at least told Anna to come over. Adeola and Hector and whoever wants to hook up tonight, what are they doing in Her birthday celebrations? He should have at a minimum check in with Her. Storming into the house with all that company! [*He was so reassuring about food, wine and cake though...* - Brain!]

She needs to find a moment to make Her complaints. The thought that makes Her extra sad is that She has been complaining about so many so much. Lately or since forever? Well, lately for sure. She cannot remember now. The thing is She feels too exhausted, too confused to corner him and complain again. And, in all honesty, happy, social mode will collapse if there is a crack to it now. Decision made: She will play on. Sooner or later She will have it all figured out and She will get Her chance to really complain.

Social mode on then and off She goes for some small talk to this person She would have rather not to have to talk to at all!

so how have you been? Have not seen you since Mark's little birthday

Yes, I know. Had to travel for work a bit so got completely disconnected with everyone.

I see, where did you go?

China. Hong Kong to be exact but broke off to check Shanghai as a deserved holiday before I came back

Beautiful! We have been wanting to go to China with Mark actually. We are getting close to actually planning it, I must say

That is what I told her! I am off to come home and bumped into her. She mentioned Hong Kong and I immediately started interrogating her!

So much so that seemed natural to grab a glass at

the cute little bar just round the corner from Mark's building. So much to share about this beautiful country

Did you take good notes, honey?

The best!

How long did you spend there?

Three weeks for work and a few more days as my break off. About a month in total in the end

Oh great. Exactly what it takes I suppose.

Yes, it's one of those you need to invest some time on

Door bell rings. She is off to the door as Mark got lost in the kitchen opening bottles, finding glasses and serving canapés.

[*At least we got some notes for the China trip out of this impromptu and unwanted birthday party. Why are more people coming though? Mark could easily have got rid of her and come home to us.* - Possibly too much wine? - *Will see*]

Hello birthday girl!

Jean, Marcella. So great to see you. Come on in.

We were on the phone to Claudia when she bumped into Mark earlier. We were planning to meet her for an update from her travels tomorrow. She has been missed!

[*It's our birthday and everyone is missing Claudia? Can*

anyone be more selfish? Are we the selfish? At least bits of the puzzle start coming into place. Still, Mark could have easily got rid of everyone and just say he had to go home to his birthday wife. Who could have blamed him?]

Mi casa su casa. Come on in. You know yourself around.

Oh hi Mark. Happy birthday to your gorgeous wife here

Thanks guys. Coming prepared. Here are your glasses!

Oh we feel so pampered [*What am I supposed to say to that?? We should be the ones feeling pampered, and clearly not the case...*]

Thank God, we came prepared too. Here is a little gift from us love [*Cute, I must admit. Better than stormy Claudia...*]

Hector joins in some half an hour later. He is completely oblivious of any birthday occasion. He is here for Adeola and Adeola alone. Possibly, same is true for Adeola, but she did make an effort to pretend this is an invitation to someone's birthday and showed up moments after Jean and Marcella with a beautiful bouquet. That finally made Claudia realise She came empty handed and a few empty promises for a huge gift were offered. Hector did not budge.

Mark had quickly arranged a catering it proves. His gorgeous cooking is not on the cards tonight. [*Will there be some of Mark gorgeousness on the cards tonight? We are going completely off script so far...*]

Catering is actually delicious and wine is expensive

and sooo good. She always admired how Mark can quickly make decisions and take care of things. She can picture him agreeing to a glass of wine with Claudia and then making all these phone calls to the guests and the catering and all. He must have had everything ready in seconds [*well, there is still this one phone call he should have made first and he did not ....* - True brain. He is still a very capable party organiser - *OK sure, and a weirdly acting husband...*]

She carries on in Her if-you-can't-beat-them-join-them mood. She is playing adorable hostess part, chit chatting with everyone and carefully and consciously leaving Adeola and Hector isolated. She has a feeling She is completely disconnected from Mark. She makes a note that Her body feels miles away from his.

Slowly but steadily, and ever so weirdly fake happy, social mood turns into real happy mood. The excellent wine picked by Mark possibly had something to do with it. The rest of the group being tipsy some glasses ahead of Her possibly made them all relax quicker. She does not have to play hostess much now, which is great. [*We still need answers, eh! I am taking notes in the background. You relax and enjoy, but morning coffee time will come!*]

Bottles of wine start piling up around the table. She is still with friends and Her man. It is not that bad. Very different to what She wanted. To what She needed possibly. It could be all that growing older theme during Her day that makes grumpy. Perhaps if Bob the Manager and that uncool stranger had not showed up She would have been more flexible with Mark's choices for Her birthday night. They can always be together Saturday night. Perhaps he has that in mind but did not a get a chance to tell Her [don't really believe this but I will keep the optimism button on for the sake of the night]. She holds on to Her optimistic thoughts yet She cannot shake off the fact that they are clearly avoiding staying together alone in the kitchen for that quick "what the hell is this" clear out. Or [the button is switched on] this is just a coincidence.

Everyone around Her is so relaxed so She ends up relaxed too. Brain is taking notes for everything in the background. She can be in the moment. All the group around Her have been discussing China for a bit and then it all went back to the usual agony: what are we supposed to do with life? She finds it a consolation that Her problems are not all that unique and She is not alone in having them.

They all share the same troubles: the complaints about the manager, some cracked communication with a friend who kind of seems to drift away lately, some relationship problems, some agony about life and death masked as anything else.

She zones out of Her thoughts and into the conversation around Her.

It's so bizarre turning a decade at this stage, Marcella notices. There was so much less stress about it when I was 29. It seemed scary stepping into 30s still but you know, very young still. No obvious signs of time. Felt like a continuum from the 20s

[Is this a joke? The universe wants to get on our nerves today?]

Totally, Mark agrees. And you know, the next stage after the 20s even felt better at points. More money, less stress about the career which started having some structure. Most people have the love situation arranged. And clearly, no visible signs of age. Huge energy, everything working [*Hector laughed at this point. Not entirely sure why*]

Has something stopped working Mark? Drunk and immature Jean picks up from Hector's laugh and points out [*Ah!*]

Mark just offers a laugh

[*This is getting interesting as we have had some misses with little (or not so little) Mr Mark down there...*]

Adeola steps in. Either to save the conversation or because she obviously agrees with Marcella's points.

What I find so unsettling is that there is no map from here. Like so far, there has been a common and quite clear script. Off from uni, first job, better job, promotion.

Yeah, same with love. Dating, finding the one, marriage, possibly children. But, you know, then what?

What is next? Where is the script, right? I seem to agree that I need one

Same here. Turning into 40s carries this confusion. Seems like we are responsible for our fate for the first time.

And disappointment! We are old enough to realise

there is no longer time to do everything. Fix everything. There are things and dreams that will get cancelled. In our 20s and 30s that sentiment was not there!

Totally.

Totally.

Totally.

Yeah and no one warns you in your 20s and 30s that unless you start mastering your own life, then by your 40s you will be forced to but with less options!

I guess that is the middle life crisis. Done much wrong in the 20s and 30s and life hits you. You have no one to blame by then but yourself and coping with that is depressing.

She can't but notice that every guest [*do they count as our guests? I am still keeping my notes for Mr Mark to explain this unannounced and unsolicited fiesta!*], every person in the room and possibly every person in the world, seems to carry the same agony. What do we do with our lives? How do we spend the gift of life and what are we supposed to do with our time on Earth?

I must admit I just carry on with what I know. I don't care what people say, Claudia clarifies. I am single in my 40s and I am enjoying it. I travel a lot and I will keep on until I have visited the whole planet. That seems like my plan. A little off script but that is it.

Fair enough, but what happens when you get 60 and it's Christmas and then you realise that you would prepare to make a gigantic turkey for a family instead of going through your travel memorabilia?

I have this covered. I will invite my brother and his 4 kids!

Everyone laughs and possibly starts thinking if Claudia's plan is actually the best

I am kind of sure what I want my life to look like in its end, I am just not sure how to make the most of the time in between. Besides, I am not even sure I will ever get there.

Yeah, that is the other thing. You work to buy the house, you go through the pain of marriage for that gigantic turkey at Christmas moment and you might never get there

Or worse still, you might have gone through the ordeal of marriage and then end up alone at Christmas because, you know, life happened and then you don't have the travel memorabilia either.

Maybe I bring some more wine, Mark offers. We need to move away from death as a subject ... [*Mark admittedly cannot handle the dark side of life*]

It is only natural on someone's birthday to think about ageing, right?

[*Is she really expecting an answer there?*]

but it's the same with work, Jean clarifies (possibly to lighten it up whilst sticking to the subject or possibly because he is obsessed with his manager) After you become the most senior in your function, where do you go from there?

Yeah, it is the same. Everyone who is older is offering advice about early career stages. Once a senior it just feels lonely.

The expectation is that you have taken life in your own hands by now and you know where you are going. You know what is best for you and you don't need that much advice and guidance any more.

Are you kidding us Mark?

I did not say I am there. I am just saying that is what is expected. Maybe we are just overthinking this.

Or maybe we got too trapped into the script in the first place. If you have been following the script blindly, you never really gave yourself a chance to think about what you want.

Oh that is interesting. So middle life crisis finds you unprepared because you got lazy and comfortable [*Lazy and comfortable, rings a bell from earlier conversations...*]

Very likely the case!

She is amazed from where the conversation is going. It feels so relatable, so painfully true. The script is there for those who are lazy and seek comfort. Successful people just crave their path, ignore the one beaten by others and navigate through life on their own terms. It takes guts, right? Some may have done it cause they had nothing to lose of course and some may have had comfort coming not from a script but from a caring family. She feels unlucky and tired. That makes it easier for Her Brain to wonder into an easier task, something more tangible to stress about: is she settling for this fun and social time when She should have asked Mark for Her proper birthday or at least to explain this non welcome surprise. She can only think he will definitely say "but you had a good time, why do you always find something to complain about". It's getting exhausting. She defers everything to the next session with Her therapist. Instead of confronting Mark, She will just give off steam with the therapist. The most difficult agenda, gets deferred usually. What the therapist clearly will not know, as Her Brain painlessly points out to Her, is why Mark put this fiesta together.... So She will pay for the session and not get an answer. [*Lazy and comfortable*?]

Someone calls Her name. She is drawn back into the conversation. Her Brain goes to sleep. Wine takes over its amygdala or cortex or what is called that controls reason. It's an interesting conversation the one going on around Her and around those bottles. Everyone seems to wonder what the successful have in common? And why they, themselves, don't feel successful. Do the successful feel successful? She is amused. She cannot really form part of the conversation. She has nothing new to add. She is afraid to admit She does not feel successful and that She has no clue how to get to success. She listens passively.

She drifts away again. She listens to the music the

cutlery makes when people are having fun. She always loved that. Made Her feel less alone. She remembers walking during the summer in the Mediterranean streets and listening to the music from the cutlery coming like a symphony from the people sitting in balconies all around the city. That music would carry on no matter how long She would walk for. Some laughters here and there. Parents calling their children. Kids playing. Feels like that, around Her at the moment.

She observes everyone around Her. They are laughing off a painful, complex, disturbing conversation. The "where do we go from here agony". She knows She won't know tonight, but it's Her greatest stressor, Her source of misery. Where will She go from here? She wonders around the room looking for Mark's eyes. She needs the consolation that She is well where She is. She does not need to travel far. Mark, however, seems busy playing host. She suddenly knows She does not just feel alone tonight, She is.

She rests Her eyes around the room again. She is not looking for anything. Cake will save them. And Her. Perhaps it's alright this is not a private Her and Mark party. But the group, even though lovely and engaging in the most interesting conversation, is just wrong. She needs Her best friend present. If She is not to be left alone on Her 39th birthday She should have the maximum best quality love available. Or is it only just a night, just a number, She makes a big deal out of. But if so, why? Why is Her birthday such a big deal for Her? Why would Mark not assume it is a big deal for Her? Is it only Her thinking like that? Other people don't care? Don't care as much?

She and Mark have been together forever now, should She not feel better about them? More grounded, less stressed? Is it Her attachment style or his genuine detachment? Why is She so sad and feels alone? Vanilla, and white chocolate and rhubarb. Her friends. They will come to the rescue.

The cake did come. Mark disappeared in the kitchen and came back with it. Lights switched off. Candles burning, melting that white chocolate away. A show happening in front of Her. For Her but despite Her. The song, the candle, the wish. The smiles. The pictures. The kiss. The clapping. The hugs. Surrounded by people. In people's arms. She still feels alone.

Her cake was marvelous. Her favorite. Somehow, Mark picking Her favorite reassures Her. This night is both pleasant and odd, he is both pleasant and odd and She needs something to hold on to. Each bite of Her favorite cake makes Her less stressed. The rhubarb, the while chocolate, the vanilla. Her friends. Well, their friends.

She carries on like that for the rest of the evening. A little like a ghost with too much going on through Her mind. She even locked Herself in the bathroom and meditated for five big deep breaths. Twenty years ago, arguably, She would have gone flat drunk to avoid the thoughts. Simple and fun [*Progress made here indeed!*]

Without Her realising it, clock shows one am. It's a beautiful clock. A gift for their wedding. The clock itself is like old school with the indices and all, wrapped into a wooden design that is futuristic somehow. A statement of how endless time is...

As with any dinner that carries into the night, there is a moment it will either go really wild and last until morning, the group will move to a night club or something, or it will tip to someone stating the obvious: "it's getting late" and then it will evaporate. When She was younger dinner nights were not that often, they cost or they seem boring but those that ever happened, would always go wild at that tipping point. There have been many more dinners in the past, mature, years that no matter how successful, end upon someone's yawn and someone picking up how late it is. Is this just a script again? Are there people Her age out there with better stamina and bigger guts that have experienced dinners differently? She needs to know. She needs to meet them.

As predicted, someone picks up it's late. It's Adeola. She wants to make clear she is not interested in spending any more time with Hector? The exact opposite? She might hope this signals a walk home together before she gets too drunk and ruins it all? They have been quite communicative all night long. She has reason to hope for a good gossip tomorrow. She smiles with the thought.

Adeola makes the first move. Hector picks it up and offers to share a cab or something. Adeola is beaming and all. That would be a good outcome of the night, if they end up together. Hector had seen Adeola in some other of their events. He has been pressing for another chance to be close to her since. There they are!

Jean and Marcella do not seem interested in moving from their seats. In fact Marcella munchies some more cake and pours some more wine! A script or not, Her getting older or not She really wishes (and needs) this little impromptu to end soon. She might get too tired any time soon and She needs some quality time with Mark. It won't look like a birthday at all without that.

Hector and Adeola leave. It takes milliseconds for the group left behind to start making comments about them or bets about their prospects. Miliseconds. Most probably Adeola and Hector picked up the wispers and the laughs. Some stubborn immaturity there...

She is not sure how and when, the group popped open a new bottle. The cork sound. Cannot be missed. It was in fact Mark who did it. Is Mark avoiding something? Is he just having a great time? Is everyone having a great time and does not care for the birthday girl? Is She going crazy? Is She too childish with this birthday girl obsession?

She is not the only one with some obsession disorder it seems. All these bottles in and Jean is still agonizing about his manager. She finds this very disappointing at this stage. A group of [almost! - thank you Brain. Back with us?] 40 year olds, at their prime, still worried, annoyed, affected, perplexed, miserable by managers. There is always someone She notices. Someone with the unfairly awarded power to control or at least affect lives. Jean is miserable during a rather happy event, wine does not seem to have won the battle in his head and this manager person is so important to him, so determinative... He is among friends, people he can potentially be happy with, but he needs to use this social occasion and this group of friends to discuss the pain, the toxicity, the misery inflicted by the life with the manager. It could of course be the case that Jean is to blame more than anyone. There are 3 more adults attending this event and all have managers. Only Jean takes this to the next level of complaining. She has had a rather disappointing encounter today (really, Bob the Manager) but She decided not to bring it up during this birthday dinner or, you know, just dinner so be it.

Is this a generational thing?

What do you mean? Jean protests

you know, the genZeders advertise they care less about managers.

Or they are lucky to have millennials as their managers, Mark points out

Yeah, millennials are emotionally intelligent and empathetic compared to past generations at least

What I do know is that I remember caring less about managers 15 years back. The ignorance, the lack of mortgage, the illusion there is plenty of time to fix everything really helped ignore the managers. Maybe that new generation is just new you know.

Could be but let's not steal millennials thunder here

The thing is, managers are unhealed, immature people who get in the way. The real question why are they the ones getting promoted?

YES! What on Earth?

And in fact the real problem is middle managers. I get to see some really skilled people at the top most of the time. But the middle field is packed with people who so obviously lack the management skillset, it gets weird.

It's a very deep social issue I guess but a quick fix would be to stop equating management to promotion. We should be able to get more money when we are good at what we do without torturing other people.

True, and we should be given thorough trainings and a real assessment ahead of getting a management role.

Yeah, people with syndromes tend to want to become managers and unleash whatever is in them as a power game. These are the exact people that should actually be banned.

Shouldn't like managers pass a test and if they are traumatised they can do something else with life?

That should be true for teachers too!

Absolutely!

One of the issues is that people hire people who look like them. So far, we have had bad managers let's say, with syndromes and all and they will hire people they can sniff are spitting images of them. It gets tricky. And we all know they processes get hacked and people end up hiring who they really want.

That is so pessimistic and dare say true it gets me sad

Then we should get better HR departments and get them independent from management!

She can feel the whole room now looking at Her. HR... She has completely drifted away from this group of people around Her. She pinned the happy face and stopped paying attention a while back already. Wining about managers seemed like a miserable state to be in [*OK, but they have been coming to some very interesting observations I must admit* - Thanks Brain, but still take your notes and come up with something to say soon. *I can opt for honesty and ask them all to leave?* - Brain!]

We should. Better HR always seems like a good idea [*that is a trick we had mastered when we were gossiping at school not paying attention in class: repeat quite assertively what we last heard... Life long skills....*]

The heated conversation calms down in the end. People around Her seem lost in their thoughts. Each on their own. In a bit, She feels them moving. She keeps the happy face pinned. She wants to scream otherwise.

Thank you Mark. We had a great time. What an evening! And all impromptu! [*Isn't bizarre people thank Mark for the invitation to OUR birthday?*]

Happy birthday sweetie! We will go crazy next year, right? Big number next year

Of course. Big numbers deserve big parties

It was a marvellous evening indeed. Thank you mate. Happy birthday dear

Thanks guys. Let's keep these regular

Oh, imagine that!

Goodnight

Goodnight

It's the two of them. Mark starts putting dishes away. He is clearly drunk. Not crazy drunk. Clearly drunk.

She wants his touch. She needs a hug. She remembers She wears that sexy crazy underwear. He does not know. He needs to be updated. She needs to leave. She wants to scream. At him!

She reserves the resentment for tomorrow. If She picks up a fight now, it will go nowhere as Mark is drunk. It will also cement Her birthday into a total failure.

As usually the case with drunk men, they get excited very quickly. She obliges. It should have been Her night after all. All Her tricks worked. She smells amazing still (not having cooked a thing really helped on that front) and that underwear is irresistible. He slowly navigates through Her curls. Has a good look at Her figure. She feels no love coming Her way, just raw animal like desire. She had missed him. She lets Herself go. She shuts down any worry, any thought and allows nature to take the wheel. Nature did. Their bodies, so familiar with each other, did what they know best. All Her senses on edge, She is Her he is him. Both let go, both know each other and go for the right places. Besides, their timing in bed has always been exceptional... If not happy, She is surely content. Satisfied. She is the birthday girl in the end.

Exhausted, She falls asleep. He usually heads to the bathroom. This time he did not. She remembers listening to him snoring before She fell asleep. She has the weirdest dream of a bird leaving a cloud and landing inside the house.

TEN YEARS LATER
CHAPTER MIRROR

She has come to terms with that image on the mirror now. She no longer dies Her hair. Time has won. She does not feel defeated though. Kind of sad Her youthful face is lost but She aged quite well still. She does not care so much for the wrinkles, not as a sign of age at least. The one think that could make Her sad are those wrinkles that mark the sad moments in Her life. The marks on Her face appearing along the cracks on Her heart. Just so that She remembers how close She got to unhappiness.

It's her birthday today. 49. There was a time She was so stressed about birthdays. So obsessed about the day and the demand to make it Her day. She realises now it was a cry for love and attention because She was not getting enough. This is not Her day, She does not need a birthday to feel special. She is special all other days and as ordinary and common as any other human. She still gets that itchy feeling that a birthday is a reminder that a whole year has gone by. She is still scared of life or of its ending (She can't even say the word: death) but not stressed. Just scared. [*Why would humans celebrate time so much? New Year, birthdays, anniversaries. Can we not just let it go unnoticed?*]

Cleanser, moisturizer, hair brush. A little blush. She looks amazing. Bizarrely, growing older and She needs less products to look amazing. All that matters is that

She is (and looks) healthy and happy. Imagine how much money She would have in the bank if She had realised that sooner!

She puts on a nice blue dress. She has an appointment with a new client. She'd better look smart and elegant. A look back in the mirror. All good, but for that hair. Impossible to tame. The mirror smiles back.

The eyes. Her eyes. Anytime a mirror is looked at those little elaborate picture processors are there. They take in the light of the world and register images. She feels comfortable with that. They seem ageless, albeit they are not. They seem rich. She feels rich. She feels there is still so much to see. So much to look at. So much more for Her eyes to register. Places and faces. Or some faces She cannot stop looking at. Her eyes are always hungry for those faces. Besides, they constantly change.

It is so funny how older She felt when younger. As if life's end was so imminent, when clearly it was not. The stress. Now the end is nearer but time is longer somehow. Now that She is getting genuinely older She realizes youth is the first end but not the end of life itself. [*We tend to get very philosophical on birthdays, don't we? Can't wait for tomorrow when it's all BAU and I am not toasted with all these ageing thoughts!*]

She looks at the mirror again. Her image is not impeccable but She feels happy regardless. If not happy, surely grateful. And She feels elegant and beautiful regardless. [*We should have bought this dress all the colors it came in!*]

She makes Her way to the kitchen.

Hey honey. Looking gorgeous.

She smiles. She kisses him.

You have time for birthday breakfast? Your favorite cake is sorted, I can do the coffees quickly.

You are so sweet! I have to meet Pete, the new client I mentioned.

Oh that is convenient. We can walk there together. Weather is nice. I am sure you will get your teeth on that cake later.

You bet.

Sure, give me 2' and I am ready. My treat.

I am spoiled or what?

I am generous or what?

This is not Mark by the way. This is Aaron. A kind, wise, supportive, warm hearted, generous, mature man. He is widowed. She is divorced.

They just found each other when it meant most sense for each. She had been dating online like crazy wanting to make life move on for Her. As always, life only happens and no one has any real control over its events. Realised that and then one day She decided to stop dating. She was going from one disasterous night out to the next, getting exhausted and the pool of Her options only got Her miserable. She remembers pouring a glass of Prosecco , deleting all the apps from Her phone and taking an oath to live a happy celibate life. She ended up crying over the entire bottle but the next morning Her decision felt right and She decided to honor it. Less than a week later She is in a cafe with Jess. Aaron is there with a colleague who happens to know Jess and they get excited and introduce everyone to anyone and they all sit together and have a great time. Started dating Aaron really soon after that. Oath happily broken. He was not really insisting or flirtatious, he seemed to want some company. So did She. Thank God they had good chemistry after all in bed and things moved on from there. No excitement, no drama, no prince hidden behind a frog. A genuine human to human moment of compatibility, joy, connection and sex.

Aaron has a daughter. A teenager unlucky to have lost her mum sooner than expected and lucky to go through it with such a great dad. She will be off to uni soon. That is music uni. Such a gifted violonist. Aaron is nothing but supportive and happy for her.

She is divorced. They are not married with Aaron but live together. His daughter is now comfortable with the arrangement. She remembers how delicate Aaron was not to force things with his daughter and not lose Her either. [*We would have messed up completely in Aaron's shoes!* - So true Brain]

Divorced. The word feels weird. She fixed a mistake but seems like it never gets forgotten. Not fully. The healing is always somehow incomplete. She always remembers Mark on Her birthday. [*Well not just on* birthdays but surely on birthdays. And there were all these days that we were thinking nothing but Mark! I felt so busy processing the same things on and on, getting nowhere!] She can't escape it. Naturally, they were together for so long. She spent many birthdays with him. It was her 39th that was the marking one though. He was holding off cracking his big announcement until after Her birthday. [Yeah, bless him for remembering how important a birthday is!]

She goes through that terrible morning after Her 39th birthday. [Again. Looking for what? -Misery.... We are looking for misery. Raw, fine misery. I am out! You will now use MY hippocampus to go through that painful memory and there is nothing I can do about it. But I do protest! There will be so much afterwards... Blood pressure to regulate, tears to release... Lord!]

The morning after Her 39th birthday She came down the stairs expecting to meet Her man. Like, Her husband. The man She has in Her life for years. The man that makes love to Her and She likes it. Her feet walk on the soft carpet. Nails pedicured. All in place. She could not tell there was a sign everything would fall apart any time soon. As She was going down those stairs, in Her silk gown, feeling sexy and processing what to tell him for that impromptu crowd the night before, She would not know She is days away from not walking on that carpet again...Until She sees that single cup of coffee... Half drunk, nothing else on the table.

Mark is all very serious looking. Very corporate. Ugly somehow. She vividly registers everything about the room, the temperature, the weather. There is this grey sky glooming through the window. The smell of recently made coffee. The chill of the morning strong on Her skin. The quietness of Mark. Bizarrely, there are no neighbors' noises coming in. She does not register. Even though She seems so acute, there is none. As if everybody knows the secret but Her. As if the entire neighborhood stands still to witness this.

She remembers his exact words. She still wonders if he carefully picked them or if they just came out of his mouth after having been trapped there for quite some time.

He said Her name and a pause. They never called each others in names. There was the "Babes", the "honeys", their little secret names. But not their given names. He turns formal all of a sudden. He really is in corporate mode.

Hi honey, ready to work already?

[No kiss. No direct look]

Honey, is something wrong?

No nothing is wrong. Not any more. But has been wrong for quite some time.

I am not sure I understand

You do

I am afraid I don't. Are you trying to tell me something?

He looked at Her as if he did not know Her. As if they

have never met before. The most empty look ever. Zero feelings behind his eyes.

She was there sitting nervous in Her chair. Not moving. Barely breathing. She would not make the work for him. He would have to explain.

I am moving out. What we have here is wrong and has been wrong for some time.

(She is shocked. Not crying. Motionless)

Ok, I am sure this is a shock and you don't like what I am telling you and you will be angry and sad and all but I know it's for the best and my decision is irreversible.

You have decided to end our marriage and you came to that decision alone? And I am 50% of this marriage but all I get is an announcement?

I just happen to be the bravest here. Deep down you agree.

That sounds paternalising and convenient!

Look, you will probably like to turn this into a fight and you might go hysterical any minute. I better be going and I will be back in a few days for my things. You will have digested it by then and come to see the truth to it.

What are you talking about? This is a marriage. Your things are everywhere, there is so much to be done even if I agree to this!

Nothing a couple of lawyers will not fix.

I can't believe any of this and most importantly how you are managing this.

Look, before this whole thing degrades too much, I will be going. You will soon see I was right.

I am in shock and your style is uncool!

- I know you won't like this and please don't start being upset and hysterical about it. We need to be adults here. I have been troubled, in so much agony and have tried to avoid this but I can't put it off any longer. I am leaving you. I am not happy in our marriage and we each deserve to live on this Earth happy. I have called Jeff and he will deal with the paperwork. He will be calling you later today. I will leave now and once you process what I am telling you we can discuss details. Split assets and move on. I am willing to facilitate this as much as possible and make it as comfortable as it gets for you. [*Every-time we play this dialogue we come to the same question: Did he expect a thank you? Still wondering....*]

She just played this whole dialogue in Her head. Again. It is impossible to count how many times She has. Back in the day, possibly more than 100 times a day. She has repeated this dialogue with friends and even strangers. His choice of words, his nerve, his audacity deepening Her wound. He did not find the strength to overcome his ego, his fear and just gave Her an ultimatum. She was left there in their kitchen alone, just wondering if they were ever together. She sat there motionless for hours. She could do nothing. Nothing whatsoever for hours. In that gown of Hers, feeling cold but feeling nothing really. She was in total denial for hours. Much later She did start screaming and crying and called everyone She could trust. Anna came in immediately. Jess too and wise Jim took the night shift. They were all gorgeous back then but nothing they could say or do would really take away the pain. She felt ruined, that the life She lived was non sensical. Wasted.

She has come to believe you can tell how good or bad a relationship has been from its ending. If there was respect and maturity and anything good in it, the ending will be a mirror of that. This is the bit that really hurts. Still. That the ending with Mark was so disrespectful. The ending annulled almost all the years She had spent in that illusion of marriage. OK, ok, not all had been bad, there must have been better feelings present back when the marriage started. It's down to immaturity and She has Her portion of blame into all this. Sure. But it hurts. Another ending, possibly, would have hurt less. [*Business idea! Teach break up at schools!* - Brain, seriously now?]

Some weeks later She found out Miranda was pregnant. Miranda would avoid Her persistently in the office. Miranda went on early maternity and resigned thereafter. Back then She would have no clue and only a couple of years later She put the two together: She saw them holding hands randomly on the street, pushing a stroller with a little boy inside.

And there She was again: She again sat there in shock, motionless and emotionless finding it hard to process: Mark resisted them becoming a family and was starting one behind Her back... How can anyone share a home, a bed, a life but keep such a secret? What is the sharing in the end? Back then Her heart, Her faith were shuttered. How would She recover from this? That was Her dominant thought back then. How would She make it? Well, maybe She would not have had but She had Jess and Anna. Mum and Grandma proved useless inevitably. Wise Jim was wise of course. She stupidly tried to console Herself reinviting and rekindling his past attraction for Her. She was so broken and selfish back then that She risked losing him. He was wise enough to know that was Her cry for help and nothing more. He helped Her the best he could and then drifted away. Who can blame him from removing himself from danger? From an unbalanced and selfish woman? The problem with broken people is that they break more things around them. They are contaminating.

[*I am really surprised we have Aaron. Pat on the back really. We recovered all that. Truly amazing*]. Truth be told She was lucky to come across Aaron after She tried putting Her pieces together. She would have pushed Aaron away had they met just a summer earlier.

They never talked again with Mark. Ever. Lawyers picked up everything that was left to be arranged. Anna would not trust Her to talk to Mark alone and she handled all the comms. They never talked on the phone, not a single exchange. A whole marriage shrunk to nothingness.

She did not make a scene that day when She saw them together. She did start seeing Her therapist a bit too often though... To this day She is so unsure who this Mark person is. She spent a good chunk of Her lifetime with this person and She has no idea who he really is. Her group of friends concluded after endless nights over wine and tissues, that She never really bothered to see. She was lost in Her idea of him. She fell in love with that idea, She got married to that idea and never fathomed the courage to look real close. To really assess what She would say yes to, commit to. Her idea of him was too perfect, so hard to live without. She preferred the beautiful lie. She needed the fairytale. Who can blame the magician when ones wants to be fooled?

Today, ten years on and he just sits there in her head, as a bad wound. No longer open or at least not visibly bleeding. But a very deep, visible scar is there. She has moved on alright. She can't forgive him though (or them both). Does She need to? Is it that She never understood? She never loved him as he wanted and needed? Possibly that. Did he care to understand Her? Possibly he tried. Possibly something was missing from the start. A key ingredient that they never procured or never learnt how to grow so just kept them apart.

In retrospect, She sees the signs. Or thinks She does. She feels the absence of that ingredient. It's funny how present an absence can feel after it is admitted. The void cannot be escaped. Cannot be filled. It is a clear absence. She spent hours in tears, litres of wine and cappuccinos and lattes, losing and gaining weight for years just puzzled what on earth went wrong in Her marriage. There is one thing She needed. That is clear. She wanted Him and Her to divorce together. As anomalous as it sounds, the healthiest ending to anything is an ending together. Alright, the decision might not be as common, as shared. But the process can be. She needed to have a saying. She needed some control, or a fake sense of control. It was Her life, Her destiny after all. Her marriage too! He summarily announced. Packed. Gone. How little he cared for Her in the end just made Her realise how little he cared for Her ever. And that is Her wound [*A Mark* - You are so witty Brain. - *Well, true. The point is Mark marked us forever*]. She allowed someone in Her life who did not care. She lowered Her standards so much, in terms of emotional expectations. She took what he gave Her and never claimed more. She carried on with the marriage patient on them not trying for children. She kept going along and She forgot to think what She really wanted and where to find it. How to claim it.

[Brain, I need to get ready for my real business thank you. - *Well then, maybe you should do just that. That is instead of thinking about rotten birthdays. Focus on our new age, new life and smile. We have reasons to!*]

Honey I am ready. You?

[*Did I process all these thoughts in two minutes, or it took a little longer for him to get ready?*]

I am babe. Off we go.

She is out first and Aaron follows and locks the house. He reaches for Her hand. She tucks Her head in his shoulder. Her favorite place on Earth.

After a few years or self-pity and impossible relationships or casual sex She got tired. She abandoned all hope to love and men. She started meticulously saving for a gap year. She needed a recharge. She came to terms She would be alone and She made the conscious decision to make the most of it. She arranged all affairs, resigned from that job of Hers and embarked on solo travelling. She visited the most exotic of places, ate the weirdest of food, slept in so many different beds. It was relaxing and deliberating to a great extent but unlike the movies that inspired Her to do it, did not work as planned. She felt Her loneliness highlighted, existential crisis kicked in hard and debt was piling up. She cried out everything, all regrets, mistakes and bad decisions but in exotic places. Possibly that was the healing She needed. The grieving She had always avoided. She came back and tried to put everything together, face the music of Her life not trying to convince the DJs to change the track. Casual sex and dating carried on. All that solo travelling did nothing for Her, and She still needed to lose Herself in a hug. She would claim it through sex and we all know look for companionship or affection in casual sex just never worked...

She took some dancing lessons, tango. Overall the therapy, the self-help books, the people She met, the places She visited, Her aha moment was in those tango classes. Her young teacher told the class her little secret: in tango, the man lets the woman shine and supports her. But she needs to know how to dance herself to shine, otherwise there is noting much he can do for her. He is strong, she is charming, they dance together and at any given moment, they can let each other go but none of them will fall. And no matter what, she shines with her figures and seems alone but always goes back to him, to thank him, to dance with him, they are not separate ever, they are a couple.

She realised She had never done that in Her coupling. So She just let Herself go and started learning how to live cause there is nothing any man could do to support Her if She did not know how to live Herself. She deleted all the online dating apps. She decided to stop looking. It took Aaron just a week to show up.

[*Well, we are happy now. Here is Aaron!* Thank you Brain!]

The bitter part, is that She still feels like She did not live the plan led ahead for Her. She did not live the fairytale. She did not fulfil the potential. [*Excuse me, why are we going through this? The fairytale of whom exactly? The potential to do what exactly? Have been looking for love all life long. I am told to shut off and close off the channel to reason and leave the heart take control over etc and bullshit! I am not the one giving you these thoughts right now* (Her Brain, is furious. Her Brain, has feelings?). *Reason and heart aligned, we like Aaron. We are glad we found him. We are happy to live in love, affection and fun. What is your problem?? Woman!*]

And what is Her problem really? Why in some ranking system the guy who betrayed Her, left Her for another woman and left the marriage childless for years gets a more shiny score and seems closer to some potential, whatever that is, to the wonderful Aaron? Because he looked right on pictures? Because he was sought after and She nurtured Her self esteem claiming She is the prom queen or something?

where did you go honey?

sorry drifted away to some dark thoughts

Well, come back here

Gladly [*There we are ... Finally*]

She walks by Aaron. He is a happy man. Easy going, affectionate. Capable. He can take care of people and things and situations. He has his scars and he did not live his fairytale either but he knows how to live, how to claim happiness for him every day. His strength is contagious, his smile is too.

His love is so deep, so full that even when upset with Her, he still loves Her. He is angry at Her, yet anger never erases love. He still respects Her and his love for Her, would never allow an argument to go too far, to hurt Her.

She always felt that level of love existed. That it was possible. She is now experiencing it. That alone is priceless about what they have with Aaron. She loves him back. She loves him as much as She can. And She tries to love him better. They way he deserves. She needs to go to love school it seems. He is a natural with love. She has all Her doubts, Her wounds, Her expectations blocking Her way to happiness. Her way to experiencing love and offering it back. When She realizes She can, She lays back with him. She is allowed to. He has Her back. She may shine alone at work, or at things She does without him, but his love is like the net that allows Her to take the risks She needs to in order to grow or to succeed. She can always safely assume that She is not alone no matter what. She really hopes She can be that net for him [*you know, we can just ask him, let him confirm how he feels and what he needs.*] They are a couple. A real couple. They are together, they make common decisions, they share dreams, they care for each other. They can be alone, they can shine alone. But the brighter they each shine, the happier they are in common. The good things multiply in their union and the bad things divide [*love maths?*] She thinks of Mark. That commonality, that shared experience was the missing ingredient in the end. They were left in their individual fears, in their individual dreams. Their love maths were wrong...

CHAPTER WORK

The meeting is with a rather ambitious guy. She tends to think ambitious people as nasty. He has so far proven Her wrong. He is structured, well intended, well mannered and with a very clear plan what he wants to do, what skills he brings in and which one he lacks and needs to hire for. He has respect for what She has to say but will not just waste money on Her if She is not doing a good job. She finds it funny, extraordinary that a client like that exists! The place they meet at also has amazing coffee! This might be a good day after all! [*I like starting a day with a good coffee, even though it feels ages ago when conscious part of me woke up. You know otherwise I am always on to something, like dreaming, or, you know, just worrying .. hohoho*]

She makes it to the cafe just a little earlier than their meeting. It's very popular this place but they manage to keep it quiet. Like it's designed for productive people. Feels like a great novel could be written here [*and maybe this is exactly what the person on their laptop by the window is doing right now!*]

She orders a flat white. A very kind guy with a warm smile and irresistibly hot built takes Her order. [*He is soooo good looking* –Yes, Brain, relax – *Well, I am reason, try reining in the other excited parts of ours*] She pauses any other thought for a moment. She just enjoys the sight. She feels like a teenager. She giggles without realizing it. He comes back with Her coffee.

Here is your coffee, smiling lady. It's not usually the case people are in good mood before they sip our medicine.

Haha, yeah that is not my normal either. Maybe it's because it's my birthday and I am so happy getting old.

Hahahaha - most probably that. Such a normal reaction to ageing! Well, happy birthday. Let me do the right thing there.

He disappears for a second. Comes back with a mouth watering slice of carrot cake. It's a massive slice. He even dusted some cinnamon on the plate to craft "happy birthday".

Wow! I love carrot cakes! This is so sweet!

Yeah - we put some sugar in it

Haha- thank you. [*He is good looking, smart and with a sense of humor! Let us not tell him how old we are - hohoho*] I am a very happy birthday girl now. Breakfast sorted so one less of life's major problems gone.

Definitely. Well, enjoy.

Thank you

Do gorgeous people develop this natural ease with humans? Like I know you like looking at me, I am never bored of it and I spark some conversation to enjoy how easily you glue on me. [*We are gorgeous too! But we just don't do that. Wow Brain!*]

So far She seems to have met a kind man and She

is about to meet an ambitious but not nasty one. Have men improved or She is better at spotting them, if not attracting them? [*an interesting observation. Can we just not analyse this and simply enjoy it? If you insist on the analysis, I will be of more help after "We sip their medicine"*]

She remembers that throughout Her life. On a good day the world seem better and on a bad day everything would go wrong and everyone would be mean. Only a couple of years back She made the conscious decision to wake up in the morning and decide to make it a good day. She trained herself to thoughts of gratitude, and She would convince Herself that the day that was about to start was a good day. It felt stupid, inconsistent, boho and what have you at first but then it proved it was paying off. She noticed the days She was actively deciding to make better were in fact better.

She no longer struggles to practice this. Has become second nature, it's wired in Her now. And as it happens, She has even more things to be grateful for. [*This is a little Chicken and egg game*].

She finds a table by the window that feels comfortable. She spreads out her iPad and a little notebook. She still enjoys writing things down in pen. [*Old Skool — happy 49th Birthday Boomer! Hohoho.* - Indeed hilarious Brain!]

Her client arrives on time. Spots Her and comes Her way.

Good morning

Good morning to you too. How are you?

I am not bad, not bad at all. You?

I got myself a coffee, do you want one too? Their flat white is just insane!

That would be lovely but don't worry about it I will order one myself. Be right back

[*Gorgeous man at the counter is a little more professional with males? Or it could be we are too gorgeous for him to have resisted us?*]

So coffee sorted and off to business

Absolutely

Oh, you have a birthday cake

Yes, it is my birthday. Somehow managed to mention it to the guy at the counter and there you are

Well happy birthday

Thanks. Had a look at your edits to the slides. Very helpful for me to understand the issues more clearly.

Well, yes I told you. My success is never mine alone. It's a collective. I want to be sure I attract and retain the best for my needs. Culture is everything.

[*Is this guy real?*]

Yes, getting the expertise on industrial psychology is key.

Indeed, I can do these things intuitively too but people trust me with their money and I need to build the culture to ensure they can trust my team too.

[*I am fully taking over sweetie now. Making money is what I do for a living. Pan intended*]

They chatted a little bit more. She got Her notes to adjust Her material and confidently run the workshops at his company. This guy is one of Her early clients. She charges less, builds the reputation and soon hoping to find a space for Her clients to meet. She could have hired one of those working spaces that popped up in the city after the pandemic but none of the places clicked. Besides this coffee shop is just so inspiring and handsomely located. [*We definitely need to think about this more after this guy pays us. Took a note*].

She did that well in the recent years. [*That decision to go consultant has really paid off. Another great idea of mine*]. She only turned consultant two years ago and has started growing into a real brand. Coming back from Her travels She invested in Herself. Felt so failed in Her marriage, in Her life that failure stopped seeming so scary. Not that She would like to count so much pain She went through as a blessing but maybe She just needed the wake up. She enrolled in classes, built up the confidence, started taking on some clients as a side gig, built a good reputation and She just started this consultancy as a real thing. Aaron was so supportive when She was not making money at first. He was fascinated when they were dating as She would describe Her adventures in consultancy. He believed in

Her. There is no competition between them. He really wants Her to succeed.

The main accomplishment is She has no manager. [*Clients can be worse pain than managers, no? - No! Absolutely not Brain*] She is a free lancer. She now remembers the little lies She had to tell Bob the Manager when She would get meetings with Her private clients booked during working hours. After a while, Bob the Manager, who once seemed an important person for Her career, someone important in Her life, someone She would call a friend for an emergency coffee for, that same Bob the Manager started feeling so irrelevant. Right now, he is nobody. She should have been more relaxed back then. She should not have crowned as "important" someone who never was.

She wishes She could go back to Jean and explain how irrelevant a manager can be when we build the confidence and our own brand. He was so obsessed with managers on her 39th impromptu party that proved Mark's procrastination to a divorce announcement. [*Possibly Jean has figured that out himself, he is also growing older after all*].

She suddenly goes through "their friends" listing them all in Her mind. She gradually fell off with them all. Some She misses, some She is glad never to see again. Adeola and Hector are married which is somehow sweet. [*The sweeter thing though is that Aaron likes our friends. They group altogether, they have fun, they share common memories. And we like his friends too*].

She finds it hard today to focus only on Her blessings. Her new age, Her new life. Bad memories seem stronger or just more in number than the good ones. The good ones are just so recent. Have not established within Her. Not yet. Why is She finding it so hard? It feels so comforting for Her to slip into the misery of the past. Like She is drowning into a gluey substance. All the gratitude meditation cannot save Her from the amount of bad memories, the amount of pain. Is She afraid? Afraid of happiness? Or just unfamiliar with it? [*Let me end this. Switches on phone and checks Aaron latest text.* She smiles - Thank you Brain!].

Ambitious but not nasty client seems content. They booked a presentation at his HQ once She is ready with the material. A few interviews after that and then the real work will begin. Establishing and maintaining a healthy corporate culture. Boy, She likes a challenge or what!

Their meeting ends. Her carrot cake long gone. Out the door. She has another meeting to go to. She has some time to waste and will take the long route through the park. Never a bad idea to check what Mother Nature has prepared for us to enjoy!

She found a bench in the park with great view. Goes through Her notes again. The plan is to meet this second client at their premises. One of the first things in Her notes is to imply and suggest the premises are boring and discourage productivity and creativity. She needs to be sure She finds the right wording [*and sugar coating!*] to land that message with efficiency. [*I have* an idea. Like, this is all I do, right? Buy them a little piece of art for the budget holder to see the benefit. On the spot. It will be harder to just describe. The visual is more convincing. Something little but effective. We have an hour to spend anyhow. - Love it Brain! Off we go]

CHAPTER THE HAVE KNOWN YOU ALL MY LIFE FRIEND

This is the moment She would call Anna and rush to the shops together.

She misses Anna a lot. It's been two years or so now without her. In fact, it's been two years, one month and 6 days. She can quickly make the calculation. She has always been good with math and terrible with loss. She remembers exactly where She was, what She wore, whom She was with, what She was saying, what the weather was like when that phone rang. It was Anna's sister. She was herself so devastated, so broken but she knew she had to call Her. Anna's whole family would have assumed She is family to them and vice versa. She remembers the feeling that Her knees could not hold Her. That Her breathing stopped. Her mind stopped too. All She wanted when She hang up that bloody phone was to lie down and stop. Stop existing. How could She carry on existing?

The route to the hospital felt like torture. The longest, hardest taxi ride ever. She could only see flashes of images of Her life with Anna. Nothing more. Any other activity was just so difficult. Calculating money for the driver seemed ridiculous.

She was standing in front of the hospital gate like a fool. She could not believe She had to go there. What was awaiting Her at the other end of that gate? Why would She ever walk into sorrow and pain? All She could think was how unfair, premature and stupid it felt that She had to walk that gate. This is for, you know, really older people. She could not be experiencing that. Why did She get a call to rush into a hospital to perhaps say goodbye to Anna? What is perhaps? Would Anna like ever leave without saying goodbye? What is this?

She kept thinking that if She does not cross those gates it will all be normal. She remembers Her legs resisting to walk. Her whole body was in denial. If She would go back to Her cappuccino to carry on talking about the weather, everything will carry on being normal, right? She fathomed all courage and made it in. She is still not sure, where She found the courage to walk that gate.

She walked in. Some kind but rather procedural nurse pointed Her to the right room. She was so envious of that nurse. That nurse could meet her best friend after her shift still, right? She could not. In moments or hours, Anna would likely not be around. How could Brain process that? Why would anyone process that?

She walks to where She was pointed at and She could see Steve. She had never seen Steve like that. Sorrow can turn our faces so ugly, so extraterrestrial, abnormal. He glimpses at Her and finding it hard to process who She is for a moment. His brain is likely too busy processing the unimaginable. She hugs Steve and asks nothing. No one would have the answer to Her valid question: why did this had to happen? It's not about what happened. Whether the motorcycle broke the red light or not, or what was Anna doing on that road and why she tried to avoid the other car and what other options Anna had. She is laying there. Crashed, unable. Inside bleeding taking her life away but showing nothing. Secretly, discretely. Anna was always like that. Calm but extremely powerful underneath. So much was always going inside of her. It was usually a burning love for those who deserved it, glorious ideas, a vision to make the world a little better. This time, the ugliest and most unfair thing is taking over Anna.

Anna's body is taking her away, switching her off, her wit and spirit and kindness and smile with it. Her Brain screams unfair. Her Heart is close to stopping.

Hey beautiful

[Anna can only nod. She has been crying.]

We are all here. You will be fine

[Anna is giving away a smile. Her notorious cynicism perhaps.]

I love you.

[Anna blinks in agreement]

Moments of silence later, having flirted with insanity, She exited the room in panic. She was ready to faint.

This is where the vivid memories end. The rest is just surreal and procedural. The funeral, the whatever.

It's been two years. One month. 6 days. She misses Anna. She needs to see Her. She needs to talk to her. Listen to her cynical jokes, gossip the world.

Hi Miss, sorry. You know where I can find an ATM?

There is this young girl standing in front of Her. She thinks She was asked a question. A black cloud seems to be hanging above Her, the voice of this young girl coming from a strange, distant place. She realises She has crossed the entire park and She is out on the High Street. She did not get to see any of Mother Nature's gifts. She only saw Mother Nature's dark side. How we are all called back to the Earth [*I need to stop this right now. I am exhausted and cannot go on about the philosophy of life and death. I will give that woman directions to the ATM and that would be the end of it!*]

Excuse me, I am not sure I heard you.

Yes, hi. They are hard to find these days, aren't they?

Excuse me?

ATMs. I am looking for an ATM. Can you help me?

Yes yes of course. Sorry, I was lost in thoughts. They have all gone digital now, right?

Totally

There is a bank in two blocks from here. Carry on straight ahead and keep an eye to the left side of the street.

Ok, great, sounds simple. Thanks and have a good day

No worries. You too

[*This woman saved us. She would never know.* - OK Brain, point taken and no more dwelling on the past for today. We need to live in the moment etc, right? - *That* is absolutely right and I am not joking about it. I am not meditating all these minutes a day to dwell on the sorrows of the past on our Birthday! We can do better!]

She is off to keep up with Her plan. Little piece of art. Her next meeting. Wrapping up with another client after a training She gave on empathy at work. Feedback session and then expect payment. [Happy days, right?]

Quite unbelievable in the end but She managed to move on. She managed to carry on living without Anna. She has stayed in touch with Steve. They are like best friends. Aaron has been very supportive with Steve too. Besides, he shares a common experience. When these two men meet She feels irrelevant. Steve is meeting Aaron at a level Aaron keeps hidden from Her. She cannot understand even if She tried anyway.

Steve has not moved on. Besides, how can you find someone like Anna to replace her? His consolation seems to be that at least he found Anna once. He had all that amazing life with her. He can't be that lucky and find that again. So he says. Either to keep himself stuck, either it's true. He has been ultra brave and thoughtful with the kids. He has been amazing throughout this as he had been amazing with Anna and with anything really. Steve and Anna just deserved more time together.

Her phone ringing. She quickly sends those thoughts away. She was on the brick of crying. She has not moved on all that much in the end...

Aaron's face on the screen among the green and red buttons. He is smiling on a beach.

Hey babe

Hi

How did it go?

Really well. I think I won him and possibly this looks like a retainer

Oh that is so cool! Well done!

Yeah, thanks. One of those days where turning self employed pays off.

Haha, yeah. More stress and more reward right?

Exactly that.

It's a little funny, right?

What is?

I cannot seem to grow fed up with success.

Hahaha, that is a really funny thought. Obvious but funny, right?

Yeah, I know. Bad times have a limit, can break you. Good times, bring it on

Bring it on babe.

You got this!

Thanks Aaron.

Need to go. You keep smiling birthday girl!

I am. [*LIAR! Well until seconds ago we were not. We keep thinking about the past and surely our ugliest moments*] Speak later.

Yes, Bye.

Bye.

It's hard to believe She has Aaron. It's hard to believe She deserves him. Her biggest fear is that Her selfish side will mess it all up. [*Yeah, very close to a mega mess up when we indulge in self pity about a fairytale that we did not live. Go check page a few pages back in this book. It's ridiculous!*]

She strolls around the city for a bit. Too many flash backs. Too many thoughts. Too many memories. She needs to clear Her head. Allow Herself to be the happy birthday girl regardless.

She found one of those shops that sell anything. Picked a little thing that definitely would not trigger the gift and hospitality policy but still lands the message that beauty around us brings beauty inside us.

She gets out of the shop and looks around. Not everything around Her is beautiful exactly but it's the city She loves. She purposefully came here with a big dream and a plan. Most of that plan simply did not work out. She is not even sure She kept wanting it along the way. Not sure the plan dropped, or She dropped it. Maybe just tweaked it and adjusted it. The city is still here. Dirty, old, magnificent and seductive. Less magical, as She is now familiar with its corners and secrets but still very exciting. She loves how it stands still and beautiful despite the times. How it still welcomes the young and the ambitious.

She remembers a time when there was a crisis and universities around the country would no longer be attracting students from abroad. Some people back then said that is fine as the young are poor and messy and loud. But in fact they fuel a city. They keep it alive. They ram across with their loud dreams, they fill it up with their energy, their hunt for mating and fun, their creativity, their laughter.

It's her birthday today, turning 49. What happens to all that creativity and energy as we grow older? A city hosting mostly the elderly tends not to be fun, not attractive, not artful. Who is to blame? Age alone? It's her birthday, She decides to spend it as She feels not as She looks. Crazy, creative and young. She starts calling up all Her friends. She is throwing an impromptu party! [*We are going crazy! And I will be the only one not having fun figuring out the admin!!! -* Just enjoy it Brain, admin is what you are best at anyhow!]

Who would She invite?

She lost some friends along the way in the past 10 years: The ones who could not tolerate Her misery after Mark. She made some new ones along the way: Those who wanted to share theirs. When She truly moved on, they started disappearing too. She always thought of Herself as non calculating person. She would not use people. She is a romantic. Yet, the happy friends were fed up of Her, the sad friends no longer did She need to use them. [*Another illusion about ourself? Let's focus on the friends we currently have no matter the reason?*]

[*Let's invite everybody we know and is in the city. Let's really go crazy! Host a big impromptu party. Some food and good wine is all we need.*]

An impromptu party. Her choosing. Her friends. No surprise. No confusion.

CHAPTER THE ONE
CLOSEST TO THE HEART
FRIEND. NO SURPRISE

Hey babe. I am supposed to call you today. What is this?

Hehe - let's skip the formalities and jump straight to the subject. I am throwing a party. Totally impromptu. Have not even told Aaron yet. Literally just came up with the idea.

Oh wow! Ok. Love this

I have some stupid show to go to.

Oh no! [*is this party a terrible idea already? It will be just Us and possibly Aaron, if he can make it after all?*]

I know babe. Don't you worry. Will get out of it.

[*Jess is a good friend*]

Well the thing is impromptuness gets tricky at our age. Life is a bit complicated. Calendars are complicated. Kids get in the way of impromptuness a lot!

This is not true. We are complicated. We use calendars and hurdles and kids as our excuse to misery. Our luxurious prison!

Woman are you a bit too philosophical for that early in the day? Are you sober or rather high on something?

Haha - no, I am usually a little like that, no?

Look, some people cannot make it but I will try.

Don't care about those

Tonight?

Yes, tonight.

Count me in. If there is will there is way.

You are plagiarizing!

Hahaha. I think this is publicly available wisdom. Free of charge

I know. Love you too. Let me make a few phones calls to make it work.

Where are we going? When?

Good point. No idea

I knew it. Call the Carlito's. Give them my name.

Oh yes! This is my girl. Will do.

I am hanging up. You know. To free the line.

Haha

Happy birthday

Thank you! Will text if I get a table

Do that.

How open is it? Do I just tell people?

Yes. anyone we know who is in the city.

Well anyone we like who is in the city I guess

Yes!

I got this!

We will never fit in Carlito's.

We will firm the numbers after we make the phone calls. One step at a time

Wise

Big kiss

Big kiss. Bye

She is dialing Carlito's next.

Hello, this is Carlito's how can I help?

Hi, I am calling to book a table for tonight.

For how many people madam?

What is the largest table you have available tonight?

Hmmm, let me see. I can get you a table for 6 people tonight. How does this sound?

Jess will be in my party.

You are a lucky woman to have Jess in your party.

That is absolutely true and it's also my birthday, do you think you can squeeze 10-12 people tonight?

That sounds like a difficult task my dear. I would hate to disappoint you.

I am sure you like difficult tasks and you crave challenges

Sounds like you do

Fair point. But mostly I find it harder to manage disappointment on birthdays

It is sad. All I can offer is I note your number and call you if I can arrange around this. A booking for six can be taken on still so it's only half a disappointment if we chose to be pessimistic or none if we keep optimistic

[*did we really call Carlito's or we are put through a yogi?*]

I can live with that and I can keep optimistic. Thank you

Can I take a name then and your number to both fix the booking and try and call in case we can north the numbers

Lovely. Thank you

My pleasure. And happy birthday

[*Are we really going to Carlito's tonight or we are just gathering "happy birthdays" by random people? Brain, be optimistic. I am sure this guy will shuffle around and accommodate us. OK, btw, who is "us"? We don't even know if Aaron can make it to Carlito's. I am sure he can, but fair point to call him now*]

[texting Jess first. She needs to say thank you and spread the excitement]

[texting Aaron]

[texting the cousin who happens to be in town]

[texting the girl from gym class with whom they tend to have fun lately]

[texting Aaron's brother]

[She can't text Anna...]

[Aaron texts back first. Very excited! - *We love Aaron, don't we? Yes we do*]

[Jess sends her collection of emojis]

She can be happy already. Her little party gathering already has the important ones. The ones who will spread the love and surround Her with laughs. Who will share the wine. Who can and will build one more night to remember. [*Brain: feels good to be loved. I cannot entirely process it but heart from a few blocks down sends some signals. Playing smart ass Brain? Yeap. You had me studying all that biology and anatomy at school. I retrieved it to prove it did not go to waste...* Ahhmmmm]

Aaron's brother can't make it. Expected. They are good fun with Aaron but as usually the case with brothers (or siblings) no matter how close and loved, they are not necessarily friends. Were they just schoolmates maybe they would not have picked each other out to bond and become friends. Family is a weird connection...

She likes him though. Good fun. The wife is super nice and the kids are alright. Quite getting along with Aaron's daughter which is important. No big deal. [*Agreed*]

The cousin who happens to be in town will make it. Not sure if that is lack of other plans or genuine desire but who cares. He is good fun. He might even be looking for a date. She remembers how her 39th birthday yielded not just a date but a marriage! Bless them. She did not make it to the wedding, as these are more Mark's group now and pretending happy around Mark back then was such an ordeal. They were cute though and invited Her out to a special dinner to mark how She proved accidentally important to their lives. Really nice gesture.

[*Not everybody is kind and grateful though.*] - True

She can list a few people She was not-so-accidentally pivotal in their lives and yet they removed Her out of their lives completely. There is one She used to have lots of fun with when She was in corporate. They would work together so smoothly, ride the same waves, share a good laugh about Bob the Manager. They were close outside the office too. Would even share city breaks when She divorced and the other was still man hunting. She then moved out of corporate and when She embarked on Her travels the whole thing faded completely. Coincidently or not that is when a boyfriend turned husband appeared for Her friend. The phone calls were not often, neither fun, the invitations for one of those glasses of wine that would turn bottles stopped, the friend even introduced Her once as an "ex colleague" to someone, not a "friend". She will never figure it out, what happened. She probably contributed and somehow pushed the person away and the person did not bother to share what the issue was. Enjoyed the comfort to quietly withdraw than loudly confront. It went as far as, for some inexplainable reason, when She crossed them with the husband on the street the other day they even pretended not to have seen Her! [*It was ridiculously clear she saw us and she even pulled the husband to walk faster past us! I vividly remember that as I was perplexed for so long afterwards!* Well Brain, most people on this planet are people we don't understand and the next large group is people we don't like. Then there is the group that don't like us no matter what we do or think we do. *Yeah, I know. We should not expect anything in return for our good deeds. - Stoic or Christian that is. - I would assume it's in all religions and schools of philosophy, as all people hate ungratefulness so need to do something about it. Usually, just accept and forgive...*]

Memories, memories and flash backs. She has been going through them all day. The good, the bad, the ugly, the happy. She choses to take a big breath and feel happy. Focus on what lies ahead for Her day. She feels happy. A calm version of happy. She has experienced a hysterical version of happy in the past. A manic, stressed version. A feeling that happiness is unstable and can go away any minute and for ever. Fragile happy. This is different. She feels calm, grounded, solid, safe. Like truly happy. Deeply content. Safe in Her skin. She feels Her skin is enough to protect Her.

She keeps making phone calls to invite people. She enjoys the buzz and the happy wishes they all share. She is almost at Her next meeting. She looks at the tiny piece of art She bought from the silly shop to make Her point. She takes Herself as little seriously possible and announces Herself at reception.

Glass and iron building, bored but forced happy girl at reception, some security choreography with guest passes, a smart elevator who knew which floor She needs to go to [*where is this going? Machines and AI and all?* - Don't worry Brain, this is for other generations to worry about. You are still top of the ladder]

Elevator dings. She announces Herself to another reception. She feels maybe this client won't budge. Too corporate to allow art to cut it through... She shakes that feeling off. She won't win the client being contemptuous to them or attacking Her self worth. That would be a ridiculous start. She clings the bag from the silly shop in Her fingers. Art might save us all. From ourselves and from AI perhaps...

She spends an hour with the client. Someone said conscious of time when the clock came to 55 minutes and someone else asked for a PowerPoint presentation to be sent through as a recap. This is all too corporate for Her. These expressions everyone repeats signaling total lack of creativity, engagement and authenticity. This is what She wants to change, this will be Her contribution to world. Make people in corporate realise how non sensical it all is, how it beats the purpose. Making money is about making something in the end.

You need the creativity, you need the fun, you need the other people.

Meeting ended and She felt it was Ok in the end. She is happy She is no longer in corporate though. Even if She ends up poor, the decision to leave the 9-5 employee life seems such as the right one. She is not sure what this meeting will yield, of course. They all seemed too wired into the corporate fairytale that She mind find it hard to uproot them. Her sponsor seems committed but each one of them individually are miles from remembering they are humans. She can't win all deals and all clients obviously, but She would like to. She does not like some part of the world and part of the wold does not like Her. [*oh well!*]. All She can do is just what She can do.

The other thing is She is not sure what message Her little art gift landed after all... [*it was a bit of a good laugh though* - That is true.] She was purposefully not blunt about it and let each one of the attendees to that meeting to figure it out themselves or come to the conclusion they wished and needed. [*Professional maturity? Lack of selling skills? To be found out... it all hangs where this little item will be when we visit them again. If nowhere, ditch the client, if hidden in a corner the message was not received, if celebrated in some well lit and visible place then we won the client and we will have our fun!*]

With all Her thinking, She is out on the street again. Checks Her phone. Messages about coming to the party or not are flooding in. Nothing matters that much tonight after all. It's Her birthday and She is planning a party.

That is about it. She has zero control who is coming or not. She will trust the process [and Aaron being there - That alone is indeed enough Brain. I know, I know].

She thinks of some more shopping. She used to buy a new dress and new underwear on birthdays. She skipped that tradition a lot in the years after Mark. In fact, on a moment of self loathing drama coupled with at least a bottle of wine She set fire to all Her sexy underwear. That was a stupid idea not only because they tend to be thirty or forty if not more a piece but also because the smell in the fireplace was terrible and the damn things took forever to burn. Neighbors complained but at least getting the fire brigade did not prove necessary. She went to live with Anna for a couple of days leaving the windows to the flat open throughout. [Was not my idea technically that one! It classifies as an impulse...]

(Texts Steve. He has been travelling a lot after Anna. He was focusing on the kids. Took him a lot to move on and still has not. Checking if he is in town. She missed him)

(Steve texts back quite soon. As if he was expecting Her message. He had forgotten Her birthday and apologized but he said he will excitedly join)

[This party is very promising! Full of love. Already]

CHAPTER MOTHER

On Her way to the shop decides to cross by Her old neighbourhood. Grandma is long gone. Grandma's closest friend in her late years [who was a lot younger than Grandma] still remembers Her birthday some times. She might call again today. Bless her.

She never decoded Grandma after all. Now she is gone and she is just a mystery to Her heart. [Quite likely Grandma would be very happy to know she is remembered as a mysterious woman! - So true Brain, so true]. She does not miss her. In a way She finds it impossible to miss someone She never truly knew who that someone was. It is the vulnerable, those who connected with us that are remembered. This is necessary for love. We need to be seen, fully to be loved. Allow to be seen and be loved by someone with eyes wide open. That is why She does not miss Mark after all. A whole marriage and he cannot be missed. He was gone from the start. He was always hiding, unwilling to connect. He started a whole new family in secret, he kept himself a secret. Possibly She did too. She did not allow any scratch to Her image with him. Would spoil the perfection She was struggling for and, in the end, spoiled everything.

Coincidently Mum calls whilst She is strolling around the old neighbourhood. She has not managed to decode Mum either and both women did not have the skill, the patience or the willingness to sort it out. However, She is no longer angry at Mum. She knows Mum inflicted wounds on Her but with time and therapy She has now identified them. She is deliberated now. She no longer thinks She is to blame for Mum's inefficiencies and She can just let it be. She used to believe it was all Her fault. That was Her way of claiming control over Her sorrow. She does not need control anymore. She can afford not to like everything about Mum. She can afford to be without Mum. She can be with Mum and not get hurt.

She can now meet Mum at whatever level Mum is and She does not have to lose Herself to get to that point. She stays still sometimes, and Mum now realises it's her that needs to walk the mile. She had been chasing Mum all Her life. Running after Mum demanding or begging for love. Weirdly [*and inevitably*] Mum reached to Her exactly when She stopped needing Mum. Mum became loving when She stopped chasing her... When She needed Mum the least, Mum showed up.

Mum is getting too old now too. She is also lonely of course but She does not care much. Mum is in control of her own life, She does not feel the need to go fix her, help her or heal her any more. She has Her own wounds, problems and moments to live.

Hi my little girl

Well, not that little any more really

Sure but you are always my little girl

[*She is getting a little bit on my nerves again. Her little girl and all* - Brain, we have accepted and forgiven Mum, remember?]

Fair enough. Where are you?

Still at the summer house. I think I will just live here. Cannot come back to the city. Does not make any sense for me to be in the city. You should sell the city house I think

Ok, we will discuss that at some point. Not sure I am ready to sell but we might rent it out instead of letting it rot. You have made up your mind to live by the beach?

Totally.

Is it safe there? You have what you need?

I do and there is the network I need here too.

That's comforting

Will you come and visit soon?

[*She is getting on my nerves. Affirmative. So needy this woman*]

Yes, will try and be there one of the next weekends. Still this month I think

[*What? Do we need to do this? Promise a visit this month? Given I am nothing but nerves physiologically, when I say she gets on my nerves we are into a total malfunction zone.* Brain you need to relax. Let it be. Don't register anything.]

That is lovely my dear

Sure Mum

Did I say the words? Happy birthday my little old girl.

Haha, yes thanks Mum

You have a plan tonight?

I do actually. Inviting people at Cartlito's

Oh! A party

Yes, a little last minute, might be just a dinner in the end

There is no such thing as just dinner at Carlito's. They say... I would not know

[*Mum has a sense of humour?*]

Someone is in a good mood today

It's the beach, the sun, the sea breeze. They do good mood to you

I am definitely coming to check it out

Can't wait my little girl.

Great. Will see you soon. Take care

Will do. Bye my sweetie

Bye

[*Well, instruction to the hands to make a note on the calendar. At least we will see the beach. Glad our birthday is not in January for instance. We might dip into the ocean even* - Silver linings Brain, silver linings. - *ho!*]

She is off to make it home. Just before She leaves the neighborhood, bumps into an old friend. They were close as kids, playing on the neighborhood streets, back when their homes were a few steps apart. They were very close physically, geographically. Sometimes for kids this is all that matters. They were never friends at heart it proved. They would consider themselves to be close before She moved out of Mum's and then the right tag to their important friendship became "old acquaintances".

Hi there, how are you?

Hey! Oh I can't believe this! I am well, how have you been?

It's been a while, right?

Totally. A few years no? If not just over a few.

Yes, possibly north of "few". You look great

You too. You don't seem to have changed much

I take that as a compliment

You should.

You look gorgeous yourself

I doubt it. Age and menopause take a toll on our bodies

Funny that you mentioned that. I would never have thought I would grow looking like my mum. I always thought I would stay hot and slim. My breasts are now gigantic and some extra weight cannot seem to shake off no matter what I do.

Glad you are so open about it. Makes it simpler to say same here.

Yeah, this is so strange. I felt I was going through that super ugly and stressful phase alone. It's such a censored subject aging. As if women in particular are not allowed to grow old.

Exactly!

It's all behind me now and it was not even that bad after all. Just, you know, weird

I know. Same, so much trepidation ahead of it and now life is back to just normal. We should have been more open and supportive to one another.

Totally. I am so relieved to have just popped this out. No idea where the urge came from but definitely something like a hidden explosion.

Yes totally. Familiar faces can do that.

I guess so. How have you been? How is your life? We seem to have jumped straight into the most difficult subject for some reason without catching on the basics.

Well life is good. Husband, kids, work. Repeat. We renovated my mum's house so we are still in the neighbourhood. You?

[*A few years back, meeting an old friend and being asked that question "what is new with you" felt like a* nightmare. *We were so broken. We were in denial that life took a turn we had not planned. A turn that was not in the fairytale script.... it was a scary moment, right?* - We are good now Brain. We are better at least].

I am good. No husband, no kids, not in the neighbourhood.

Really, what happened with Mark? You were like America's sweethearts you two, I would never have expected you are not together.

Well, I guess we put on a very elaborate varnish hiding the cracks. I have Aaron in my life now, very happy.

[*Is she looking at us in disbelief? Does she feel sorry for us?* - So be it Brain, she cannot know. We do]

I am glad you are happy

[*Please brain of hers, if you can hear me under some secret code of the universe, don't ask any more questions, we are not that close any more, right? And I would rather go home*]

Thanks. It's my birthday tonight actually. Want to join us at Carlito's? A good chance to meet my new life

Oh happy birthday. Thanks, such a lovely invitation

[*It will take her two seconds to use her kids as an excuse not to come. Wait for it. One of them is sick, I bet!* - You might be right there Brain, let's see. - *One, two...*]

Not sure I can make it my dear. Will need to check if Peter can stay with the kids and the oldest has been a little unwell this morning so it might be a stretch.

[*Hilarious! She will now say "some other time" or "but maybe we can catch up any time soon" but without offering her number or a specific time frame. One, two*]

Maybe another time? But soon?

[*Brain is laughing*]

Of course. Well great to catch up. Just show up if you change your mind

Will do.

Be well my dear.

You too.

[*Some people are clearly unhappy but like it when they have reasons to trick themselves to feeling superior to others. Only because they have kids, for instance, and the other person does not. Women have been tricked to see other women competitively and compare their beauty, husbands and kids a lot. Women should just sister up. Instead of hiding infertility agony and menopause, they should just support one another. - Great observation Brain. - Let's go sister up a bit and make this a better world? Let's do that*].

She walks down the block. More phone calls and texts for tonight. She feels the girl of the day! As Jess predicted the ones who love Her will surely try to make it. They are excited to hear Her voice and willing to share Her moment. [*There are also those who just like parties.*

– The fun ones are very welcome too.] The others bring up excuses, sound more procedural and social. Very kind but bored. [*I am keeping a list. I am checking it twice... - Brain... - We will invite only the good ones to our 50s! Cannot afford lukewarm friendship, not any more! - Fine Brain, make your list... by all means...*]

She smiles to the thought. She thinks about Her encounter just a while ago with the girl She used to be friends with from the neighborhood. The realization She needs to open up and sister up more stayed with Her. Drop the competition and the judgement and just be there for others. Or maybe not even that. That is a role too. Just be there with others. Just be present emotionally. Just allow the heart to be there. There seems to be more of that in men's friendships. This useless competition between women, where does it come from? [*From harems, when they had to share that one man to feed them all? - Have we read that somewhere Brain? I don't have a vivid recollection reading about it but seems very probable and plausible, no? - We should definitely do some research on this. Yeah, might even write an article or the sorts. - Totally! - On the (hmmm long) to do list! - Spare the cynicism Brain, please. - Cannot promise but will try*].

She is back into the city centre now. Startling shopping windows all over the streets make Her remember the original plan to go shopping and She knows just the place for it!

Fouty nine. Her body is no longer slim. She has a good diet, some dissent frequency at the gym. She is no longer gorgeous by some glossy magazine standards. But boy, She feels gorgeous. There was a moment in time She would even fit those glossy standards marginally and back then, She would not feel gorgeous. Her audience in men was always sizeable and She did not feel gorgeous. Her audience is now possibly shrunk to Aaron only but, inside, She feels gorgeous. This is what matters. Not necessarily what is, but what feels.

[*I guess we were obsessing with menopause terror because of those glossy standards? There were no gorgeous, happy menopausal women anywhere to look at and feel comfortable.* That is true Brain, in our modern world feels as though joy is reserved for the 20 somethings and in fact, the beautiful only among them...]

She visits Her favourite boutique in town. She is not after a dress to impress situation. This is not about them, the audience, Aaron or anyone. This is Herself offering a gift to Herself on a birthday. A little refresher to Her style. She just decided She will even have it wrapped as a present even though She is paying for it. It's meant for Her.

The owner of that boutique knows Her. She welcomes Her with a big smile and warm wishes for Her birthday when she realises. There is an obvious reason this boutique is a huge success in town. The owner cares or at least shows to care for the client. Remembers names, tastes, life events. There are other places with good clothes, better even. Clients need their pampering and are ready to reward it and stay loyal to the place that offers it. Right? [*Are we shopping or going through a marketing 1:1? It shows we are fourth nine, we are still shopping in brick stores.... Hohoho.* What's with the cynicism in Her head? *Possibly an alert not no get carried away but that happy feeling and spend it all on a pair of boots.* Thank you Brain, but use something else than raw cynicism next time? *Copied that, fair point. All those self love books you had me reading...*]

This boutique is just paradise on Earth. The perfect closet any girl would want. Well, any girl with Her taste. She seems 100% compatible with the shop owner. That is a rare kind of happiness... It is made up like part of a home. Decorated as if you are visiting a friend for tea party. The owner is just so clever if not canning, that allows you to shop things online and host a coffee / tea event with your friends who also bought things online and open the boxes together and make decisions which bits to keep or return. Those returned are more often than not, replaced on the spot with something on the premises! Great sales! [*I need more time with the brain of this shop lady...*]

The decoration lately has an artistic theme. As if you enter a loft in Manhattan where a wealthy, classy, gorgeous friend lives and lets you try on her clothes. Interesting art on the walls. Mirrors that could be art themselves thoughtfully scattered around. The shop owner even pays someone to do a study of the lighting in the place. It's an average size store and ends up giving the impression of a huge place. The changing rooms are the best detail. They are rooms. Real rooms. Two. There is a secrétaire in each, a lamp and one of those art looking mirrors. Naturally lit by a massive window overlooking the high street. In any other place, the changing rooms are a miserable, artificially lit part of the store. By the time you try on the pieces in this place, it already feels owned. In any other place the changing rooms are so bad, people end up not liking the clothes or even not liking themselves. In this store, the pieces look simply gorgeous when tried on. And then, if the piece looks beautiful, it's hard to part with, no? And even though the trick is obvious [*I confirm*] it works! [*I need to have a conversation with that department who falls for these things. Amygdala or something? They are falling for all those marketing tricks so consistently and then I need to work extra time to find the money they spent....*]

– So what are you looking for?

[*We should not say a gift to myself. This will keep the options offered unnecessarily on the high end of the budget.* Good call Brain]

Something to refresh my style a bit.

A little gift to yourself for the day?

[*ok, we can't beat her sale tactics. Drop it but remember, it is us doing the choosing. Don't fall for the compliments. That changing room is not our room! Stay sober!*]

I am sure the gift part is taken care of today. A nice dress would be great [*Look at us! Took us years but we have now mastered the art of staying sober whilst shopping!*]

Haha, of course. Lucky you.

There are some pieces that only came in this week. Really gorgeous and I have one in mind that is great for your body type and style!

[*Of course, she will say she has the perfect piece. In all fairness, part of her success is not pushing anything to anyone. She has an eye for what looks good. That is another secret to her success. Or just part of that one thing that makes a sales person keep their clients long: measured honesty offered in a the most calculated installments but peppered with flattery. Counterintuitive as it sounds... (some) honesty in sales works*]

Ok, can't wait!

Have a look around and I'll be right with you.

Damn... She immediately spots a pair of earrings She fell for. She has a thing for earrings. Ever since youth. Her collection is rather impressive. Most are picked while traveling. An easy thing to carry in that luggage and a cute way to remember the times in interesting places. She smiles, as a few of the travel memories start flooding in Her head. [*it is quite a storm in here!!*] The pair She fell for is colorful with blue and red dominant somehow. It's that kind that stays really close to the face, almost glued to the lobes.

[*The clever shop owner is coming our way. She holds a few options. Careful!*]

Oh those earrings [*Careful!!*]. I could not resist them.

I only bought two pairs and then kept one for myself. I should be making better choices with the merchandise!

Hehe. They are quite incredible. They decorate the face without taking over it. That is a balance hard to hit with jewelry.

Totally. I know exactly what you mean. I brought you these dresses to try on. But if you go for that pair, you might just stick to a little black dress to impress. They are not that expensive in any event. But the dresses I had in mind are somehow too colorful and will dump the earrings away.

(The clever shop owner is already in the little black dress section of the store as she gives that little analysis)

I see what you mean. Yeah, you need to chose whether your impressive item is the dress or the earrings.

Exactly.

She tries on the dresses anyhow. Just for the fun. She will not fall for them. They are gorgeous. Her mind is set. It's the earrings. She has a classic black suit at home to pair them with. She even tries on the little black dress She knows She does not need and would never buy. She realizes on a quiet morning, on her forty ninth birthday, that in the end, shopping is about women turning back into girls, playing around in a closet. Trying dresses on. Looking at mirrors. Welcoming beauty and the joy that comes with it. Ending buying the item or not is irrelevant.

They all look gorgeous. But my mind is too set. I will only go for the earrings.

Wise choice. We had some fun though didn't we?

Indeed

Let me put them in a box for you

Thank you. I am sure I will back for one of those dresses soon anyhow

Hehe - they are the kind you fall for, I know.

The shop owner gives Her a generous discount because it's her birthday [Brick shopping still pays off Brain. This discount would never be as generous online! *Ok cool. Do you want me to publish an article on the FT about it? I kind of hate online shopping myself. Too much strain on just the eyes, with the rest of the senses to no use. Touch for instance is very important when buying anything with farbric.*]

She puts that little box in Her bag. Maybe not a token of travelling in space this time, as so many of Her earrings pairs are, but possibly a token of travelling in time.

She exits the store with the little box in Her bag. Where should She go next? [*Off to the hairdresser's. That hair is historically impossible to tame...*]

The hairdresser is not necessary really. She is just offering Herself some pampering as She is now past the pure vanity age. It's all about feeling good not looking good these days.

Back in Her vanity days, She would even sacrifice time and well being, health even for some looks. Painful hair, toxic dyes, high heels. Pain as a currency of beauty seems stupid now. It should have felt silly from the start. Wondering who was the first to introduce pain as necessary trade off for beauty and why did other people follow? Why did women oblige to such a terrible trend? [*Philosophical on a birthday again?*]

That age until mid-thirties when looks are important, is actually because it looks good. The funny thing is that until mid-thirties or just a little earlier, women don't realise youth is there to make them look good regardless. The make up is silly, there is the gorgeousness of young skin itself. Health and youth just radiate. Why on earth do we even bother to enhance nature's wonderful creation? We don't put make up on trees, we just look at the beauty of the forest. We don't put make up on a sunset, we just let our senses get lost in it [*There was a trend to add filters to capture nature's beauty but it was soon replaced by the no-filter trend. I guess no-filter should have been the trend with people's faces and bodies all along... hundred years before social media and smartphones. But humans seem wired to masking, to a lie, to altering reality to better cope with it.*]

Past Her mid-thirties now. Past Her mid forties enve. As She grew older She never stopped taking care of Herself, never stopped caring to be healthy and kind to Her body but the agony of the looks faded. Inevitably. That battle is lost no matter what She, or anyone, would do to hide being past youth [*There is no way back from* the wrinkles. In the end, though, they don't seem to matter. They seem so scary before they settle on the face but then, once they are there, they are just part of us. Just existing same as the rest of our body. They don't define us. They just came about because we lived.] In the end, as long as She did Her best for Herself, She would no longer care what She looked like to other people, what other people thought, or what was expected of Her. That also saved Her a great deal of vanity money. She is now at the hairdresser's practically for the fun of it all and the head massage She thinks She needs and deserves.

Hello Dear, how are you?

I am well, you?

Do you have an appointment?

No but here for a quick blow dry. Can you slot me in?

Hmm, let me see. Can you wait 20-30'

Yeah I don't mind.

Oh that is lovely. Take a seat for me and Samantha will call you

Awesome. You have a new edition of any of the glossy magazines? [What??]

But of course my love.

[They still make them? Are they not illegal by now? Brain, are you being too brainy?] Cool. I fancy their impossible world every now then

Not impossible dear. It just comes with its price

[*Deep. Unexpected in a hair salon*] Aren't they all?

A couple of glossy magazines, dwelling on what the stars have lined up for people born under Her sign, and a hair massage later, She is ready to head back home. Hair tamed and no large shopping bag. She did well.

She is taking the longest route possible. She looks at shopping windows. Goes through the park. She lets Her eyes rest on the ugly beauty of Her favourite city. Trees, then tall buildings, then the sky, then some beautiful balcony, then some inexplicably complicated narcissistically designed building, then a beautiful store, then a funny kid, a well dressed person...

She makes a stop at one bookstore that makes great coffee too. It's a magnificent concept between a bookstore, a lending library and a coffee shop. She borrows a random book and sits to enjoy it together with Her well made and extra large cappuccino. It's a story of a girl who looks for happiness. She looks in all the wrong places, wasting time and only making her agony worse. She is carried away by Her book and possibly, without realizing, laughed out loud at one of the hilarious narratives. The man sitting at the table next to Her either annoyed or amused, cracks a conversation.

you need to tell me about that book. I should be sure to order another coffee when you leave and be the next to get hold of it. Is it really that funny?

[*are we being hit on at age forty nine? Oh la la. So*

proud. Brain, it could still be the book. Not everyone is flirting with us. *I place you a bet on that and meanwhile will keep my version of the truth, thank you*]

Hi, it is actually. Did not realise I was loud. It's one of those that soak up the reader and got carried away.

Yes no worries. This is not a library after all, right? It's a reading room with a coffee place or a coffee shop with books. Not sure. A caferary, if I am allowed to play with words and coin the term!

Ha, that is an interesting new trend. Good you came up with a name for it.

[*He smiles. In THAT way. He is definitely flirting!*]

Will see. Only time tells if trends last.

That is true.

So what is the book about?

It's about a girl looking for happiness. In all the wrong places obviously

But of course. That is where we all look for happiness... Pretending we are wondering where it is when in fact, we are just afraid to find it. Cause, you know, what do you do with it once you get it?

Yes that is exactly what she does

I hope the writer of the book has realized that looking for happiness is not the quest of an answer.

How do you mean?

Happiness is asking the question not looking for an answer.

Meaning?

If you ask yourself, what do I need right now? Yourself will tell you. And meeting your needs will leave you happy. Same with your loved ones. You can spread happiness by asking them. What do you need? What can I do for you? They will tell you. If you can meet their needs they will be happy.

[*Did flirting man just say something deeply profound that solves all our problems? I will create a headache to keep focused in the background and digest this. You do know I am interconnected to the gut, hence the terminology, "digest", right?* - Brain, you are losing it here. Stop]

This is quite something you just said. Truly, I am not sure the writer of the book will get there. The heroine seems quite far from it.

But it's rather simple, isn't it? Think a sequence of days where all your needs are met, or that you at least tried to meet them all and picked your battles, sort to say. Would you not feel happy? But how can you get there without the first step. Without asking yourself what your real needs are.

This is really interesting.

I mean it's so simple we can play it as a game now.

If I ask you, what do you need right now? You will immediately connect with your body and soul to look for the answer, won't you? That is practically what it takes. And if you want to keep your husband happy, I assume you are married?

[*ok, definitely flirting*]

Well, just go ask him. My love, what do you need right now? It's his birthday for instance. You are troubled to find him a gift. All that guesswork to keep him happy and mark the day special. Ask him. What do you need on this special day? What can I do for you. And if you meet that special need he replied to you with, he will be happy. Guarantee. Simple

It definitely makes a lot of sense.

It takes courage to be open to the answer. Hence, we hesitate with the question. What we need might be difficult, uncomfortable, costly. What our loved ones need might be that too. So we skip the question, we come up with a handy random option instead and then wonder where happiness is.

But what if coming up with the handy option was our need.

[*Proud*]

Well that is not a tricky issue. If you reply the question you just asked with a yes, you are in happiness. If with a no, keep on asking. Oh need to go (the man's phone blips, as like an alarm clock)

Of course, don't let me keep you. It was a genuine pleasure. Thank you

Same here. Enjoy your book

Or my Q&A

Or that. Have a good day

You too.

She never picked that book back up. She kept sipping Her coffee, going through various questions in Her head. She is trying to figure out if it is indeed as simple and if fear of the answer is the only sabotage keeping Her away from her own happiness and from making those She loves happy.

[Jess texts. Checking about tonight]

[You will never believe what just happened.]

[What?]

[I met the happiness guru at the coffee shop]

[Really? What does he look like? Some old man with boho shirts that smells dope?]

[Stop it. I am serious]

[Can you be?]

[Oh Gosh]

[Fine. What did he say and he is the happiness Guru?]

[That happiness starts with a question. What do I need? Or asking a loved one what it is they need]

[And what do you need my loved one?]

[I want you to stop being cynical and listen to what I write]

[Fine. Wish granted. What an interesting guy! I am so happy you came across him! Happier now?]

[Yes thank you. What is with you?

[I am stressed about making you happy tonight and if Carlito's got you a place.]

[<3]

[Did they?]

[Yes I have a tiny table of 6]

[How many are coming?]

[Not sure yet. There should be space at the bar. I am sure they will fix us close to the bar, as I mentioned a birthday. I think...]

[Fine. It will be fun. Promise]

[I know. Not worth worrying about having fun. Fun will come to us]

[You are very much into philosophy again. Could be that guru of yours]

[Could be. But think about it]

[Will do. Wine tonight will help. Xx]

[xx]

She is heading home. She will prepare a light meal, relax and later start getting ready. She has a few texts to answer. Some little work to do at the back of Her meetings and some thinking and dreaming too.

Home is cute. Aaron was wise as some point in his own healing journey to move house. Too many memories there. Made it impossible to move on. He got closer to the city. His daughter was getting older and made more sense to come closer to the city action too. He did not sell. Possibly a bad financial decision, but She cannot blame him. He is not ready to part ways with the past completely. He might never be. She will never replace his wife. She is not supposed to. They still share a child. That is a such a strong bond even with someone who is gone. She wishes Aaron would not carry that wound. It is no longer oozing, but it's there. A very deep scar.

She can absolutely call their home, theirs though. Meticulously decorated by all three of them. She brought in pieces from all Her life. They fell into place somehow, looking good with the new and the shared. Same for Aaron. Somehow the mess makes sense and everything looks good next to another. Art, memories, expensive, luxurious and DYI in a beautiful mess. [*That is what it looks like when I scan inside our soul too, let me reassure you.* I am sure that is the case Brain].

CHAPTER PARTY

The night has come. The table is booked. Everyone who said will be there is. These gatherings always come with mixed feelings. [*The food and the wine will take that away*]. Aaron picks up the shadow in her eyes. Kisses Her forehead and asks what's wrong [*Ok. The food, the wine and Aaron*].

There are people I miss tonight, that's all

Of course you do. That is fine

I know. It's all normal and fine. It's just a little sad. A little unfair

It's big sad sweetie. You need to allow some room for that. There is room in my arms if you want

Oh those arms baby. My favorite place on Earth. And trust me I have travelled.

I know! There is this long list of places you have already been to and now you no longer fancy going back. When are we going to Jordan babe? I want to go with you!

[*We love what he does. This balance between perfectly understanding our feelings, allowing room for them and then giving us a witty joke just to keep the drama in check*]

Seems like we have some travel planning to do.

She is then left to mingle with Her group for a second. A nice lady that She has never met before, comes Her way.

You look lovely my dear. Happy birthday

Thank you! Do you have a drink? Are you taken care of?

Yes I am all good. How can someone not be at Carlito's?

You are so right about that. I am so happy they managed to squeeze us in.

Pure luck?

And a gorgeous friend with good connections

[*should we not find out who this woman is? - Yes, Brain, can you come up with a nice question that will not put her off or insult her? - Keep the chit chat and I am working on it in the background. Where is that chatGPT when you need it??*]

Do you come here often?

Oh, there was a period I think I was investing my salary in this place

Haha, I can imagine. There was a period this place was so hot! Talk of the town if not of the County

That is true. Absolutely true

But that was like 20 years ago

Yeah, I guess we were the lucky ones to have lived through its golden age. In fact, us two, we met here [*Oh, the plot thickens!*]

Interesting. Tell me your version

Yeah, I don't assume you remember. I was chasing Jim back then. A very futile chase, Jim was rather in love with you. I would go where he goes and then would never imagine he would hang out at Carlito's. But I think it was your birthday again so there he is. At the end of the night, I made a fool of myself and came forward at him but he rejected me. You actually tried to make me feel better with some philosophical analysis. I was ultra drunk and hated you but then I needed the consolation so took it. I left town for many many years. I am here of a conference, some colleagues wanted a show around town and thought of Carlito's. Did not expect to find you all here and that it is your birthday again.

I see. A full circle.

Yes.

Jim is not in town. I guess it would be different to see him too.

The Jim I was chasing no longer exist, I am sure. He might not remember me either.

So what are you chasing in town?

Just my younger self I suppose. I felt very young seeing you at Carlito's after all this time.

I see what you mean. I chase my younger self often. There are only certain people that offer that connection. I found love much later in life myself and I often wish my younger self could have been around. Albeit, the truth is, most probably my younger self would have destroyed it all.

I totally see what you mean. It's a consolation chat once more but I better head back to my colleagues and my current self. It was great to see you.

Thanks for a glimpse of our youth.

Of course. You mentioned Jim is not in town. Please tell him Debbie says hi.

I will.

Where are you in life now? Shall give him some info if he asks?

We are all married and remarried and parents to different set of kids at this stage. Aren't we?

I guess so.

It does not matter.

Got you.

Well, enjoy, great to see you.

Thank you. Thank you for coming to say hi.

[*I have been going through all the events of all our birthdays at Carlito's. Cannot spot a moment of us that she described* - It does not matter I guess. Feels good going through these memories still. Feels good of thinking of young me and young Jim and all our love troubles. They seemed enormous back then. - A *classic "what if" of ours, that Jim thing. Shall we not go out to dinner with him and dig into the past bravely?* - What is the point? - *What is the danger?*]

Daydreaming, lady! Where are you?

Oh you are exactly the person I needed this right moment Jess.

How come?

A Debbie came to say hi from across the room. She has moved out of town but happens to be here today. One of her last days before leaving was my birthday at Carlito's back when we were, what, twenty four?

Of course. I remember.

You do?

Yeah, she was crazy for Jim. She ended up ultra drunk and crying for him that night.

I have no recollection.

Yeah, we were trying to comfort her for a while. She ended up crashing completely and a couple of people from our group put her in a taxi and took her to her flat. Have not seen her since.

Interesting. Total blank about it.

I can imagine. It was your birthday and you were obviously carried away from it all. Besides, it was one of the first birthdays of yours when Mark would make his mark.

That I remember for sure. Life is so funny. She was obsessed with Jim. I with Mark.

Jim with you.

Everybody says that tonight.

It's true.

The point is all of us made such a fuss about something that seemed so important, insurmountable, back then. And now we are just cool and have it all behind us. It's so bizarre of a feeling.

We are still glad we made a fool of ourselves for love at least once, right?

Haha, for sure. She also said something very true. She came over to say hi in order to connect with her younger self.

I see what she means.

Yeah. I am so lucky though. I just need to look at you and here I am. Feeling young immediately. I can feel the shared continuum.

I know honey. I love you too.

I love you so much.

She lets Herself rest in Her friend's hug. Feels great to be loved in a continuum. She was hoping that would be Her marriage but feels alright to at least to have the blessing right now. From someone. At least one person in the world connects with Her with a love, a friendship so deep and strong. That feels alright.

Jess lets Her mingle again. Say Her his, pay Her dues.

Enjoy the company of everyone who showed up. Her party is not different to any other party of hungry people, who like the company of one another. There is good food, good wine, good mood. Maybe that is all it takes for a birthday. Jokes, giggles, catch ups. Nothing too much. Fun does not need anything that special. It just happens.

She takes a comfort break for a second. Heads to the ladies' room. Carlito's are one of those places where the restroom is a such a concept. There are luxurious mirrors everywhere. Literally everywhere. Dimmed lights. Awesome smell. Funny doors and all sort of deeply philosophical messages framed on the wall. Looks Herself in one of those mirrors. The wrinkles are now stubborn. Nothing can make them go away or really hide them. They are there no matter how blunt Her facial expressions are. Some tricks like the blunt facial expressions worked for a while. They would hide the wrinkles, along with anything else. She has some expressionless, feelingless photos from the era She was trying to hide Her wrinkles. [*Worst pics ever!*] Her most beautiful photos in the end are the ones She is allowing to show Herself. Happy, fool, angry or annoyed. These are the ones that got framed in the end.

Looks back in the mirror. She is glowing from the fun, the love and the wine. Her hair eternally messy, now a little grey. She is a lot of things. She is also not a lot of things. For some it's too late. She is not a mother for instance. She made that choice Herself a while back. She is not sure She regrets it but She surely feels a sting in Her heart every time She thinks about it.

The morning after Her thirty ninth birthday She would not believe the million things that happened. Mark left. She was there alone. But did not feel alone. She started missing Her period. For weeks. She thought it was the shock. The sadness. Messing up with Her badly. It has happened before. For instance, when She had wasted some time with that abusive boyfriend from college calling Her fat and ugly... [*Anyway, we left that guy soon enough. Should we had left Mark sooner?*] A few weeks in and Anna suggested She takes a test. She did.

She was anticipating that moment for years. The moment She would finally be the one taking a positive pregnancy test. She always thought it would be a moment of ultimate joy, celebration and happiness followed by cuddles and kisses and hugs. Instead, She was in a messy bathroom, alone, looking at those two lines crying Her soul out, feeling lost, alone, stressed and miserable.

She never called that creature a baby or a child. She wanted to become a mum but not like that. Not alone. And with all that terrible finale not by him. The thought of raising a child that came out of a wound moved the needle for Her decision in the end.

She ended up feeling nothing but disgust. No fear, no joy, no agony. Disgust. She played with the thought of becoming a single mum, of giving Herself the chance to motherhood but back then, surviving felt more important than growing. She took the test at around week 5 and by week 6 it was all gone.

There are people She misses tonight. Surrounded

by love, Her wounds, not necessarily healed but taken care of, allow Her to think there is room to start giving back. She misses Anna tonight for sure, but maybe She misses that creature too. If not that baby, Her option for one. The scariest part of growing old is not the intimacy of the end, is the finality that some options disappear. As we grow old, choices solidify our path and there is less time to undo them.

She finds funny how 10 years back She was so scared of menopause and when the menopause got cancelled by a pregnancy She could not feel relief. She realised back then that fear of menopause was not enough of a ticket to motherhood for Her. She needed desire for it. She should have wanted that child, not just fear its absence. We act out of desire. Fear usually immobilises us, cancels any action or any progress. Creating, a creature, needs desire. Menopause still seemed better. Easier probably. Today She realises it was not that much on Mark to blame. She was not ready. She did not want it. Maybe if She did more, Mark would have been engaged. He did become a dad after all. Just with someone else. She did not become a mother. So maybe it was Her not inviting Mark enough all along.

Sometimes She thinks of calling Mark. Of calling everyone She ever met in Her life and talk to them. As strong feelings evaporate, what is left is usually a sweet, calm sense. Some sort of gratitude for the growth She achieved with each person in Her life. She has no room for remorse, anger or pity. Self pity. She can only feel alive and grateful. She shakes the thought of calling everyone in the middle of the night. Besides, it takes two. She cannot just assume that other people found that sweet, calm state. They have their own reasons to hate Her and might still do. Their own reasons to be afraid to talk to Her or embarrassed in the end. Does not matter. Those who need to look for Her will and if She needs to look for others, it will feel easier. Possibly necessary. Maybe later, maybe tomorrow, maybe some other time She will make those calls...

[*Seems I need to bring some balance between the misery and the joy here. We are going back and forth all day.* Point taken.] She goes back to the dinning area. Some younger people around them are really into the party. This place is famous for brightening up after dinner. All these young people around Her, flirting, promising, dreaming. Full of options.

[*Excuse me! We are not that much older. Relax. What on earth are we going to say in our seventieth party?* - It's only that some options are no longer available. Some people are no longer available. That is what the younger don't have usually. They have not experienced the limitations yet. - *We cannot travel back. Can we enjoy the now? You had me reading all these books about living in the moment and meditating. Apply what they were all about!*]

She goes back to Her table. Aaron is focused on Her.

Hey. You alright?

Yes, yes.

You are lying?

She avoids him and goes straight into her "favorite place on Earth"

Babe, what can I do tonight to make sure you are happy?

(She remembers the man at the "cofferary". She has not realised She got that close to true happiness after all. [- *Oh wow. We are loved and we finally realise it!*])

You don't need to do anything my love. I am happy. I am the happiest I could be.

She lets Herself into the music. She joins that crowd of the younger. She might not have all the options lined up for Her but She has the comfort and the confidence that some of the choices She made, some of Her decisions played out well. Those that did not, made good lessons, protected Her from worst, propelled Her to the good. Some others just made good stories. Youth does not have that confidence. She smiles at the thought [*finally!*], spins around on the dance floor, let everyone that loves Her hug Her, touch Her, dance with Her. Feels great. Feels alive. She has love. She still has time. Youth does not have love established. Not solidified yet. Smiles at the thought again. Counts Her blessings and steps out to catch another negroni. Sips the redish liquid in pure joy. Like life, Her drink is bitter, sweet and gives an icy shock as the ice rock hits the lips, but is damn good after all.

It's two o'clock. Crowd is thinning. She says a lot of goodbyes and thank yous. She grabs Her gifts. She likes them all. Aaron offers to put everything in the car. She takes a look around the room. A young couple are kissing.

Clearly a date that will end in one of the twos' place. She sees a girl somehow alone and sad. She calculates if She should go talk to Her. She might have a nice story to tell at someone's birthday some many years from now... Who knows. Decides to let the young girl live the drama. Maybe she needs that to grow out of it. Thinks for Herself that She no longer has much drama in Her life. She no longer needs that. That is surely a blessing of not being that young any more....

Aaron is back ready to go. Gives him a gorgeous kiss. Hugs him tight. She is not drunk. She is happy. He smiles back. He is happy. Jess promised to drop by for breakfast or better brunch the next day to catch all the gossip. Life seems perfect. She has spent so many of Her birthdays at Carlito's. Most of Her youngest ones. She walks out of Carlito's tonight somehow thinking this might be the first time She is out of that place genuinely happy. She might not need to come back anytime soon.

CHAPTER MIRROR

She is getting ready for the big day. Aaron's daughter is turning ninenteen. She will be out of the nest after the summer.

She puts on a nice comfy dress, spends seconds on a beauty routine, glimpses the mirror for obvious mistakes in Her appearance and disappears downstairs. She is tasked to make the cake.

Hello

Hello, birthday girl

Hehe, thanks (they squeeze each other in a big hug)

I am making you a chocolate cake

OMG! My favorite!

I know sweetie. It's not a random choice of recipe at all!

I am sure.

Shall I help you?

By all means.

(Amidst the sound of the mixer machine and the dirt of the flour scattered around like a magical misty cloud She hears the most wonderful words)

You know I want to make a confession.

A confession?

(The young girl is not looking at Her, pretending to be laser focused on the eggs she is beating)

Yeah, like a love confession

That sounds intriguing (She pauses anything She was doing. Cannot even remember what it was. [*This cake might never happen from the sound of it. Let me start thinking of alternatives*]

You know I was so unlucky to lose mum and for a while I was miserable and angry. What I could not see is that I am lucky to have you. You are not Mum but you are not to blame for anything. I see that now. You are not replacing her. You are here with your kindness, your love to just carry on living. The gap I used to feel is shrinking. I used to feel I am left with just Dad but seems I have more than Dad still. I still miss her, but I feel less alone, less empty. I have you too.

Sweetie. You cannot imagine how beautiful it is what you just said. I understand it's not a comparison. Can I give you a hug?

Please

They hug tenderly. Through their bodies a lot of other things are told and settled. The girl leaves a chocolate mark at the back for Her dress. This will be discovered a lot later and it will make Her smile. The biggest smile since She was thirty nine years and six weeks old, making that decision in the clinic to end Her options to motherhood. She got a funny second chance. Like a half chance. She did not mess it up. Maybe She mega messed up back then. Maybe that decision was a bad one. Who knows. No one will ever tell. Sometimes feels like a bad decision still but Her life does not feel bad. Just that decision. [*And many more*].

So I am a real adult now. Off to uni. Any tips?

Stay where the love is. Move on from where it is not. As fast as you can.

I can see what you mean.

Please keep that in mind.

Anything else?

Well, your youth will end and spend it wisely. That is impossible but keep that in mind too. And if you find that your youth has ended and I am not around to remind you, end of youth is not end of life.

The girl looks back at Her, perplexed and overwhelmed. Stays silent. Somehow puzzled. [*Too difficult for a nineteen year old to understand*]. Possibly someone had told Her a similar thing when She was nineteen. She did not understand. She had to go through life Herself and then figure it out. [*This precious shortcut to wisdom we are all doomed to ignore. It escapes us. Every time.*] Likely that person alarming Her, would have been Her Dad. Her gorgeous Dad. If not, it would have been wise Jim. Maybe we are not all equally doomed to ignore wisdom... Jim never did...

They carry on with the cake. There is chocolate literally everywhere now. Egg shells, empty packs. The beautiful mess of baking. In Her culture there is never baking for the bad things. Baking is always a celebration. Ever since She was a kid, an empty pack of flour, broken egg shells and piss of tissue that used to cover a block of butter would be a signal of happiness. She is looking around at Her messy happiness. She put good ingredients together, destroyed them with fire and a beautiful cake came out. Could have been ashes. She got lucky. Again.

The girl is melting some more chocolate and asks all details about how to decorate the cake. Aaron is coming through the door all smilie and carrying boxes for his girl to pack away.

[*Do we think the girl could process what we are telling her?* - Unlikely Brain but the seed is planted. - *Are we dropping the idea to urge her to freeze eggs for some piece of mind? That is some wisdom we could have benefitted from I reckon!* - Let's leave that for the cake at her twenty ninety birthday. If she still needs it. With so much love around her, maybe she gets wise too].

She picks up the phone. She wants to call wise Jim and tell him she loves him. Wants to tell Mark she no longer hates him and hopes he is happy. She wants to call Mum too. To tell her she messed up big time when she was raising Her but She got out lucky in the end. Aaron drops the boxes and gives Her a huge hug. Aaron seems to need Her today. She loses Herself in his hug. She forgets about the phone calls again. Maybe she will forget all regrets one day and just live. She has so much time.

THE END